Trinity

A Novella by
Rachelle Jarred

Trinity
Copyright and Disclaimer

Dedication

I dedicate this fifth novel to all of my family and friends and readers who have supported me in many ways. I have come too far to turn back now. I thank God for blessing me with this amazing gift that I am able to share with the world. I love you all and I am so grateful to have you all on this journey with me as I live out my dream.

Prologue

Hey y'all, my name is Mia Jacobs. I'm originally from the Bronx in New York, but I been living in Washington, D.C. since I was maybe about 18 years old. I came out here to attend Howard University and I was excited. I was finally going to be away from my mother and be able to do whatever the fuck I wanted to do. I must say that I have experienced a lot while living in the nation's capital. I have seen people get stabbed in the club, police running up in people's houses like it ain't shit, and most of all, I experienced the most heartache that would last a lifetime. Now, years down the road, all I can say is fuck those niggas that I came across in the past seven years. I'm only twenty-nine but I am in love with the man of my dreams. Yeah, that's right; your girl is in love. His name is Lamar Washington and he is a few years older than I am. I met him when I was twenty-five and have been in an on again off again relationship. The thing about Lamar, he likes to mess around with other women. All my friends call me dumb and tell me I can do better but I don't want to. My boo will come around. As a matter of fact, I gotta get ready because he about to be home.

/ /

Yo, yo, yo what's up, y'all? I'm Lamar Washington but everybody calls me "L." I'm originally from Trenton, New Jersey and had moved to Maryland about four years ago. I was single for a brick and now I got this bad little shorty named Mia and I kind of like love her cute crazy ass. I met her one day she was at the bar, and she was telling me that her boyfriend left her after cleaning out her bank account. He skipped town with all her hard earned money, however she earned it. Anyway, I seen her across the room and went over to put my charm on her. Not sure if it was my game or my boyishly good looks that won her over, and it doesn't really matter now, but I was happy as fuck. After a few dates and spending nights with one another, we decided to make it official. Everything was going good until I seen an entire different side of her. This one time she came to my house, I

Trinity

had another girl in here and she went wild. She asked me why did I do it and I came back at her like what you doing popping up at my spot like that? She beat the damn girl up and broke so much shit in my house. That crazy broad even smashed all the windows out of my brand new Porsche. She ain't talk to me for a few days but came right back when she calmed down and started missing daddy. She knows she can't live without me. Years later, me and baby girl still going strong for the most part. Little does she know I got a little surprise for her when I get home.

//

Hey ladies and gents my name is Sonya Jamison and I'm Lamar's side piece. I'm from the nation's capital Washington, D.C. and the city runs through my veins. Lamar and I had met when I was actually dating someone on his team. The dude I was dealing with was just a runner and Lamar was the big man on campus. We were all hanging out one night getting drunk and high. I caught his attention, even though he was with Mia that night, and I had followed him when he dipped off into one of the rooms. And, of course we fucked that same night and after that. I ended up breaking up with whatever his name was and gave my all to Lamar. Now, I think shit is about to hit the motherfucking fan and some more shit. He told me he was tired of keeping me in the shadows from Mia but truth be told so was I. After we did our little session, we went back to the spot where everybody else was and acted as if nothing had just transpired. I continued to watch him the entire night. I saw him whispering something into Mia's ear and moments later, she strutted over to me, asking me to come to their house for a late night rendezvous. Only thing is, that one night turned into a romance for Lamar and me. In all honesty, I wanted them both and I was hoping Mia would be open to a polygamist relationship full time. I ain't greedy but to have the best of both worlds is a girl's dream. Hope this turns out how I want it. We were already here and there was no turning back now. Lamar grabbed me by the hand and we walked up the stairs to their little apartment.

"Hey, Mia, baby I'm home," he yelled throughout the apartment. "I got a surprise for you." She came from out the kitchen and looked at me with those beautiful green eyes that caught my attention at the club that night...

Contents

Prologue ii

Chapter One Three Years Later 1

Chapter Two Day Out 9

Chapter Three Baby Maker.. 19

Chapter Four Five Months Later 39

Chapter Five Three Months Later 53

Chapter Six Thanksgiving Day 65

Chapter Seven The Big Fight... 83

Chapter Eight The Hospital 95

Chapter Eight Secrets Surface... 105

Chapter Nine Merry Christmas 120

Chapter Ten Happy New Year.. 129

Chapter One

Three Years Later

"I am sick and tired of both of you bitches keep going back and forth with all this damn fighting," Lamar yelled at the top of his lungs.

"Don't you talk to me like that, nigga. You must have lost your damn mind," Mia yelled back. "If anything you should be fussing at Sonya."

"Excuse me?" Sonya interjected.

"Yeah, I said it bitch. You don't belong here. If you weren't here in the first place, Lamar would still give all of his attention to me goddamnit."

"Perra por favor Eres tan estúpido y no te das cuenta de lo estúpido y tonto que te ves. Él me ama tanto como tú," Sonya yelled at Mia as she made her way across the room. Mia, who's originally from the Bronx, never backed down and was coming to meet her in the middle. Lamar jumped up from the couch and stood between the two women.

"Now cut that shit out, Mia. And, Sonya, chill out with all that Spanish mess because nobody knows what the hell you're even saying." He looked into Mia's eyes as he continued. "Now, you wrong for that. Sonya is as much as family as you are. We agreed to bring her in so we could all be together, right?" Mia nodded her head as she rolled her eyes and folded her arms. He looked towards Sonya. "Are you happy with us, Sonya?" She nodded her head and copied Mia's stance. "Alright then, now I want y'all to kiss and make up."

Trinity

The two women looked at each other and their hearts made their emotions go soft for one another. They both leaned over Lamar and began to kiss one another. Their tongues were entwined together as they grabbed the back of each other's head and kissed harder. They could feel Lamar's hand on their backs and gave him their attention. He kissed Sonya first, and then kissed Mia. Before you knew it, they were in a three way kiss, tonguing each other down. Lamar was getting aroused and they saw his manhood rising inside of his boxers.

Mia pulled his penis through the slit in his boxer briefs, prepping him for the head she was about to give him. Sonya continued to kiss his lips and neck as he rubbed on her breasts, drawing her brown nipple into his mouth and gently biting down. Mia got down between her man's legs and instantly began to lick and suck all over his penis. Within moments, it was covered in her slob and going deep into her throat. Watching her do this was turning Sonya on. She joined Mia on the floor and laid on her back, placing Mia's pretty pussy right in front of her face. She licked and sucked on her clit, putting her fingers inside, making her juices flow all over her hand. She sat Mia on her face and Mia grinded into her face until she squirted all over her mouth. She dropped Lamar's dick from her hand and turned her body around and began to eat Sonya's sweet kitty.

Lamar looked on in amazement from the sofa as he admired how his girls were taking care of each other's needs. He moved the sofa back a little and got behind Mia and entered into her warm vagina. As he did so, Sonya sucked on his balls and enjoyed the tea bagging he was giving her. After Sonya squirted all on Mia's face, Mia turned around to kiss her man. He took turns fucking both women for an entire hour until they both got his hot nut shot up inside them. They kissed each other and apologized before going to take a shower. While they did this, Lamar ordered their food for dinner and told them he was gonna shower after they finished. As they showered, all Lamar could hear as he walked past the bathroom was water, laughter and kissing. He smiled to himself knowing what was about to go down in the shower. Mia and Sonya were gonna be in that shower for at least forty-five minutes to an hour. He decided to roll up a couple of blunts for him and his girlfriends so they can be ready for later.

He went into his safe and pulled out one of their many jars of weed. He chose to smoke a little OG Kush tonight, which was Sonya's favorite. He grabbed his papers and funnel and rolled up four nice jays. He pulled out his phone and ordered them some food from America's Best Wings on Uber eats. The app so they will be delivering in an hour. "Goddamn them niggas is slow," Lamar said aloud. He shrugged his shoulders and just placed the order. As he finished rolling the last blunt, the girls were coming back into the room wearing their camisoles and boy shorts they got from Pink the other day.

"The shower is waiting for you, baby," Sonya said Kissing Lamar on the cheek.

"We already cleaned the tub and put your new bottle of body wash in the shower for you, too, baby," Mia replied following Sonya and kissing his other cheek.

"Cool cool, thanks, boos. I'm getting ready to hop in and wash my balls and shit. Listen out for the delivery man because the food is on the way."

"We got you, babe," Mia said taking the blunt from his hands and grabbing a lighter from the nightstand. Sonya grabbed the ashtray and they smiled and skipped happily back to the living room to watch their ratchet TV. Lamar shook his head as he laughed at them as they jumped on the sofa and smiled and puffed on the blunt. He went and got into the shower that his girlfriends had running for him. He hopped in and exhaled because they always had the water just right for him. He was in the shower for about twenty minutes before he got out and oiled up his body and threw on a clean pair of boxers. As he exited the bathroom, he saw both of the girls hopping up and racing to the door.

"Hey, ladies, how y'all doing?" Lamar heard a deep voice say from the doorway.

"We're fine," they replied in unison.

"Did you guys order Uber eats?"

"Yep," Sonya said reaching for the bag of food.

"Wow, you two are gorgeous," the delivery guy said.

"Thanks," Mia said as she attempted to close the door. The guy pushed the door back to continue to spit game at the women.

"Are either of you single?"
"We're together," Sonya chimed in as Mia just stood there snickering.

"Oh, so you two are lesbians? That's pretty cool."

"We're actually bisexual," Mia responded.

"Yeah, and they both are my girlfriend and belong to me," Lamar replied coming up behind them and opening the door wider. Mia handed the bag to Lamar and grabbed Sonya's hand. He smacked both of their asses and they laughed then made their way to the kitchen.

"Oh it's like that?"

"Straight like that," Lamar said. He pulled the delivery guy closer so he could whisper in his ear. "These are my girls you hear? Don't ever let me catch you trying to talk to them again because if I do, it's not gonna be pretty." He handed him a twenty dollar bill for a tip and slammed the door in his face. Just as he was making his way to the sofa, the girls were coming back out the kitchen with their bottles of water and a couple of beers for their man. He handed them both a tray of food and they sat back and continued to watch Black Ink Crew.

/ /

Later that night, the trio of lovers was lounging in the bed watching episodes of House Hunters and enjoying each other's company.

"I wish we could get a big house like that," Mia said as she ran her fingers up and down Lamar's midsection.

"So do I, Mia," Sonya replied mocking Mia's hand motions.

"Look now don't start that mess you two. I already told y'all we would move to a bigger place when the time is right."

"And when exactly will that be, Lamar? Because you have been saying that for the past year or so now." Lamar grabbed her by her throat and leaned into her face.

"It's gonna happen when I say it's gonna happen. I don't do shit when y'all want me to. I do shit when I wanna do it and if you got a problem with that, you can fucking leave. Do you understand me?" he replied through clenched teeth.

Sonya looked on, wanting to say something but she didn't want to end up in the same predicament. So, she just sat quietly and simultaneously looked back and forth between the TV and her two partners.

"Yes," was all she could muster up to say as he gripped her throat tighter. He placed a kiss on her lips and then released her after a few seconds. She laid there pouting for a few minutes then hopped up and ran into the bathroom when she felt the tears welling up in her eyes. Lamar didn't like when his girls cried and she didn't want to hear his mouth anymore tonight. She grabbed the washcloth she used for her face and washed the tears away that stained her skin. She used the bathroom and went back to the room. She saw that Lamar and Sonya had taken up more space on the bed, including her spot that she was just occupying. She walked over and stood next to the bed.

"Where am I supposed to sleep, Lamar?"

"Since you wanna act like a spoiled brat, I'm gonna treat you like one. You go lay your childish out there on the sofa bed and I will see you in the morning." She continued to stand there and glaring at him. "You didn't hear me?" he asked sitting up in the bed. That's all she needed before she put some pep in her step and left the room. She grabbed a blanket and pillow from the hall closet and made her way to the living room. She pulled the bed out and turned on the television. She didn't really wanna watch anything in particular. She turned on the Bounce channel and turned over and silently cried.

Why does he always treat me like a damn child? He never treated me like this until Sonya's enchilada head ass moved into our place. I should just leave. But I can't live without him nor do I want to live without him. So many thoughts ran through Mia's head until she fell asleep, listening to the ending of Spike Lee's Snipes as she dozed off to La la land.

Around three in the morning, Mia heard light footsteps across the floor and felt someone pull back the covers and climb under the covers with her. She knew it was Sonya by the sweet smell of her raspberry shower gel and Herbal Essence shampoo. Sonya threw her arm around Mia and pulled her close to her body, kissing the back of her neck. Mia could feel her hormones beginning to rise and started to moan softly. Sonya moved her hand down between Mia's thighs, and slipped her fingers into her panties. She rubbed her clit gently getting her aroused and Mia was grinding her body into Sonya's. Mia moaned softly and Sonya sped up her fingers and her kisses until Mia couldn't take it any longer. She turned over to face her female lover and removed her hand from out of her panties. She sucked her juices from each one of Sonya's fingers before kissing her and climbing on top of her.

She kissed her lips, then her neck, before making her way down to her breasts, sucking and licking all over them and marking her territory. She kissed her stomach and belly button before removing Sonya's panties and diving in between her thighs. Sonya arched her back with each lick that Mia had given her pussy. After she came a little, she pulled Mia up and kissed her again and placed Mia on top of her. They felt on each other and rubbed

Trinity

their pussies together, moaning loud enough to be heard through the silence of the night. Mia excused herself for a second then came back carrying one of their dildos. She put one end inside of Sonya and the other inside of her, and they went to work. They sexed each other until their bodies were worn out and bruised around five o'clock. They laid cuddled together as the morning sun peeked through the cracks of the blinds.

//

"Wake up, girls," Lamar said opening the blinds and clapping his hands loudly close their heads.

"What the fuck?" Mia said as she sat up on the sofa bed and rubbed her eyes.

"What's going on, baby?" Sonya responded as she stretched and yawned before sitting up next to Mia.

"Y'all have been sleeping too damn long and y'all need to be getting up. We about to go for a ride," he replied grinning.

"It's way too early for this mess."

"Come on, Sonya. Let's just hurry up and go so we can come back and go to sleep," Mia said nudging her and throwing the covers back.

The two women watched as Lamar ran back outside and got into the truck. They both dragged their feet to the room as they looked for something to wear for the day. Sonya settled on a minidress and sandals while Mia decided on a short skirt, tank top and sandals. They washed their face and brushed their teeth. As they were grabbing their purses and phones, they heard their man leaning on the horn signaling them to hurry up and come outside. Sonya locked the door as Mia hopped in the front seat with Lamar. They scrolled through their social media feeds as they rode along the highway. After being cooped up in the car for almost half an hour, they pulled up to big house with a two-car garage. Lamar pulled up into the driveway of the house and they all hopped out. The girls scanned the street and noticed the neighbors were a little ways down the road. They all walked inside and Lamar gave them a tour. After the tour was completed, they all stood back in the foyer.

"So what y'all think? This shit is hot right?" he asked cheesing from ear to ear.

"Yeah it's dope," Sonya said looking out the window.

"So whose house is this?"

Lamar reached into his pants pocket and pulled out two sets of keys, handing a set to each of the women. "It's our new house. Welcome home, boos."

They looked at each and squealed, hugging one another before running over to him and jumping all over him. To thank him for this gesture, they both kissed all over him before dropping to their knees; showing him how much they appreciate their gift. They thanked him right there in front of the big picture window that could be seen through if there were anybody that had possibly passed by and looked in.

They were so happy and couldn't be more excited. They couldn't wait to decorate their new place. They got back in the truck and smiled harder than ever as they drove away, observing the house as they looked out the back window.

Chapter Two

Everything had been going fairly well in the household of the lovers. Lamar went to work on the block as he usually did and the ladies did what they did best-sit at home and take care of the house. A few days after they moved in, Lamar surprised them both with matching Dodge Chargers. Mia had an all white one with purple interior while Sonya had an all black one with pink interior. The two women loved their cars and was even more happy because they were paid for straight out with cold hard cash. Lucky for them, Lamar's drug business was always doing well and they never had to work or want for nothing.

"Oh my god, girl. What you feel like doing today?" Mia asked Sonya as she climbed out of the pool and sat on one of the beach towels. Sonya was lying back on her beach chair soaking up the sun and reading a good book. She closed her book and gave her attention to Mia.

"I honestly don't know, baby. Maybe we can go shopping. What you think?"

"That's cool with me. I'm going to go call Lamar and let him know so he can get his assistant to drop off some money."

"Cool. As slow as his ass is, we're going to have time to shower and probably watch a couple of movies." The women broke out into laughter as they left from the poolside and headed inside the house.

While Sonya took her shower to wash the chlorine from her skin, Mia called Lamar and told him their plans for the day. He informed her that his assistant would be there in a couple of hours and that he wasn't going to be home until Saturday because they had to make a run. They exchanged 'I love you' to one another before ending their phone call. As Mia finished up, Sonya was finishing up her shower. She cleaned the tub out for Mia then headed to the room to join her.

"So, what did Lamar say, Mia?" Sonya asked as she moisturized her skin.

"He said Shyne would be here in a couple of hours and that he wasn't going to be home until Saturday."

"Well, that's cool. It's only two o'clock and that gives us a few hours to shop and do whatever and then maybe catch a movie and grab dinner."

"That sounds good. We should go to one of those lounges in DC."

"That's cool. You think we should ask the girls if they want to come with us?" Sonya asked.

"Nope, not at all. We already gonna see those bitches Friday night when we have our ladies night," Mia laughed. She stood to her feet and made her way over to Sonya. She moved her hair away from her face and kissed her lips. "Besides, I want you all to myself tonight, baby."

"I'm with that," Sonya replied welcoming Mia's lips and kissing her back. She could feel her juices starting to flow inside her pussy and gently pushed Mia away. "Uh uh, baby cakes. I already had my shower for the day and I don't want to get dirty."

"How about just a little lick?" Mia begged.

"No, babes. We can save it for later."

"Alight, man, if you say so. Let me go take my shower and get ready."

"Please do," Sonya said before giving her one more kiss and sending her on her way. After covering her skin in lotion, it was now time to figure out what to wear today. She knew she wanted to wear some tennis shoes at least. She walked into her walk-in closet and looked through all of her jeans and shirts. She couldn't decide on any jeans so she figured she would just wear shorts. She grabbed a thong and a pair of denim shorts, fastening them and admiring how good they made her ass look in them. A little bit of her booty meat was hanging out the bottom but she didn't care. She loved her ass and so did Lamar. She put on a pair of fresh white no-show ankle socks and pulled her new Air Jordan 11s that Mia had gotten her this past Christmas. She went back to the closet and picked out a white and black PINK shirt to match. After giving her outfit a once over and approving it, she grabbed her necklace and her bracelets and her sunglasses. She was in the middle of a private photo shoot when Mia came back into the room.

"Girl what on earth are you doing?" she asked giggling.

"Don't do that, boo. You know your girlfriend likes to take pics before she leaves the house."

"I know and so do I. So, don't take so many right now."

"Just a couple more," Sonya replied as she continued to try and capture the right angle for a perfect picture.

Mia just shook her head and laughed at Sonya as she moisturized her arms and legs. She, too, decided to wear shorts today. She chose to wear black shorts that hugged her ass just as nicely as Sonya's shorts with a plain white t-shirt and the same Air Jordan sneakers that Sonya had on. She put on her jewelry and a little bit of makeup and lip gloss before adjusting her weave. After she approved of how she looked, she joined Sonya in the mirror that covered one of the bedroom walls and took pictures as well. Their shoot was interrupted with the ringing up the doorbell. They both jogged out the room and could see Lamar's assistant, Shyne, through the glass of the door.

"Hey, Shyne," they both said in unison as they opened the door for him. He hugged them both and watched their asses bounce up and down in their shorts as they walked away. They all gathered at the table and he handed them a suitcase. They opened it and were welcomed with hundreds of dollars. Mia ran to get their tote bags and came back, and they loaded all the money into them, totaling around $15,000 apiece. They didn't even leave anything to take back to Lamar, not like they ever did or he ever expected them to. They both gave Shyne a hug and grabbed their car keys before they all left out the house together. They watched as Shyne hopped into his Lincoln Navigator and drove away, beeping his horn at them. Mia and Sonya decided to ride in separate cars as they headed to Tysons Corner Mall in Virginia. That was about to be one hell of a drive from Bowie. They started their Chargers and followed each other as they drove through the streets, making their way to the interstate and peeling down the highway doing 75 miles per hour.

/ /

Mia pulled into the parking lot and surprisingly, Sonya found a spot right next to her. They hopped out of their whips and locked their doors. They walked into the mall with only one thing on their minds-spending money. Their first stop on their list was Armani Exchange. They split up in the store so they could both get a gift for Lamar. Sonya walked through the store, getting cat calls and stares from the guys in the store. She smiled and waved instead of being rude to them and continued to scan the men's accessories. One dude was real bold as he brushed up against Sonya and cornering her by the belts.

"Damn, nigga, you don't know how to fucking say excuse me?" she replied pushing him away from her.

"My bad, sexy, I was just trying to get your attention."

"Well, your ass definitely got it. Now what the hell do you want, my guy?"

"I wanted to know if I could get to know you. What's your name?"

"Sonya," she replied with noticeable attitude and a slight eye roll.

"Um, okay. Are you going to be busy later? Maybe we can hook up and chill or something. What do you say?"

"I say she already has plans for the evening," Mia said walking up from behind him and standing beside Sonya.

"Oh damn, its two fine women. Hey, ma, I got a friend for you if you want to meet him. I mean, damn, unless y'all wanna make it a party and I just have both of y'all?"

"We already having a party together later," Mia replied grabbing Sonya around her waist and slobbing her down.

"Oh, it's that kind of party, huh? Hell, I like that type of party."

"We're gonna have to pass. We already got a man, love," Sonya said as she grabbed Mia's hand and headed out the store.

"Fuck both y'all bitches. Y'all weren't that damn cute anyway," he yelled to their backs. They never looked back as they cracked up laughing as they left out the store. There was no need for them to even look back and entertain his foolishness because they knew they looked fucking good, and so do all the other patrons in the mall that were make googly eyes at them.

Mia checked her watch and saw that it was almost four o'clock and they hadn't bought anything yet. So they decided to hit up the jewelry store and the shoe store to grab some new kicks and heels. The two ladies walked into Pandora and admired all the fine jewelry that laid nicely in the display cases. The white sales lady saw them and paid them no attention.

"Excuse me, excuse me," Sonya said waving at the lady trying to get some assistance for her and Mia. The lady glanced their way and ignored them as if they were just a couple of flies on the wall. "Did you just see that?"

"Yeah, I saw that shit, Sonya. I should go over there and smack that bitch." Just as she was heading over to the rude woman, Sonya grabbed Mia by the wrist and stopped her in her tracks. They watched as two white females that looked to be their age come into the store and the lady jumped at the opportunity to help them. Mia and Sonya exchanged looks at one another as they watched on as she showed them numerous pieces of jewelry. Fed up with the counterperson's disrespectful attitude, Mia snatched away from Sonya's grip and marched over to the other end of the counter.

"No, Mia, wait," she said trying to grab her again. She was too late and Mia was approaching the women. She pushed the white girls out the way and stood before the sales lady.

"Bitch! I know motherfucking well you seen us in here first and calling you for assistance."

"I'm sorry, miss, but I don't assist your kind," she said bluntly with a look of disgust on her face, as she turned her nose up at Mia.

"My kind? Trick, have you lost your mind?" Mia said. She didn't even give the lady time to respond as she reached across the counter and punched the lady square in the face. She grabbed at her until she had a handful of her long blonde tresses. The two young ladies backed away and fled the store so they wouldn't be next.

"Mia!" Sonya yelled. Sonya ran up to Mia, trying to release the grip she had on the woman's hair as she pounded her face. She managed to get her fingers from out the lady's scalp just as a young woman came over.

"Ma'am, ma'am, is everything okay?" she asked trying to calm the situation between the women.

"No everything is not okay. This bitch right here not trying to help me and my girlfriend with her racist ass."

"Mrs. Dawson! I am appalled at your behavior," the young lady responded as her face turned beet red. She looked back to Sonya and Mia and apologized for her manager's behavior and offered to assist them.

"I don't think I want anything out of here anymore," Mia said as looked back at Mrs. Dawson who was holding a handkerchief up to her nose as blood ran freely.

"Ma'am, please, let me help you ladies," the young sales women begged. Sonya nudged Mia and told her it was cool and to let the girl help them.

They were in there for all of twenty minutes and walked out dropping seven thousand a piece on new jewelry for themselves and Lamar. Since the women didn't call security or anything on them, the two ladies each gave her a thousand dollars for her help. Her eyes grew and she thanked them graciously. Sonya had slipped the women her number and told her to call if she wanted to hangout sometime. She was cute and she and Mia only hung out with bad bitches. Mrs. Dawson looked on and looked saddened because it wasn't her that received the sale or the money. Before leaving out the door, Mia bucked at Mrs. Dawson and caused her to damn near jump out of her skin. She laughed hysterically as she headed out the store with Sonya pushing her and giggling, too.

"I'm hungry, Mia," Sonya cried as they continued through the mall.

"Me, too. You wanna get shoes on Friday when we go shopping for our outfits?"

"That sounds cool. So are we gonna grab something quick out the food court or what?"

"Sure. I don't think I wanna be starving until we go out later. Besides, that's a long ass ride back out to Bowie, shit."

"Girl, you know that ain't no lie," she responded laughing. They decided on grabbing a small bowl of orange chicken, fried rice, and chicken egg rolls from Panda Express. After they paid for their items, they looked for a table to sit at. For it to have been a weekday, it was so damn packed with both teenagers and adults alike. Mia tapped Sonya on the shoulder and pointed to a table off towards the end of the food court. They rushed over and sat down before somebody else could get it. Sonya bit into her egg roll as soon as she sat down and Mia cracked open her bowl and started to dig in. As they were grubbing and discussing the details for their ladies' night on Friday, they were approached by a group of young dudes.

"What's up, green eyes, how you doing?" one of them said as he sat down next to Mia. As soon as he leaned over in her direction, she was smacked with the smell of musty underarms and cigarette breath.

"Um, hi," Mia responded as she could taste the stench in her mouth and wiped the water from her eyes.

"What are y'all names?" another one asked.

"My name is Shante and her name is Cassie," she smiled. Sonya smiled right along as she held back her laughter. Those were always the names they used when ugly guys were trying to hit on them.

"Nice to meet, y'all. Are you here with your man, Shante?"

"Naw, not today. I'm here with my girlfriend."

"So I see. Your girlfriend is bad."

"I know that's why I'm with her."

"And that's why I'm with her," Sonya chimed in winking her eye at the dude.

"Oh, y'all some lesbians, huh?"

"Bisexual. We got a boyfriend."

"Say what. Y'all on some freaky type shit but I like it though. Put my number in your phone and hit me up sometime, baby girl."

Mia rolled her eyes and pulled out her phone. "What is it?" The dude gave her his cell phone number and told her his name was Black. He told her to text him so they could all link up and she promised she would. That was a lie. They never gave their number away to anybody, unless they were looking for a playmate and that's when they gave their numbers to females. They parted ways and the girls finished up their food. All they could do was laugh at the confidence level the guys had.

/ /

They arrived home at almost 7 o'clock and were so tired from all the walking and driving, that they decided to just chill out in the house for the rest of the night. They took turns taking showers like they did before and threw on some comfortable pajamas and some ankle socks. They sat on the chair and Mia searched for a scary movie while Sonya searched through her Uber eats app to order them something to eat.

"What you in the mood for, Mia?" she asked.

"I could go for some pizza and wings."

"You're such a fat girl," Sonya responded as she closed the Uber eats app and opened up the Domino's app. She placed an order for two medium pizzas and an order of ten Buffalo wings. She paid for the food with her apple pay and saw that it wouldn't be delivered for almost an hour. She rolled her eyes and threw her phone down.

"I decided we should watch 'The Conjuring'."

"You know that damn movie scares me, Mia. Why we can't watch something else?"

"Because horror movies are freaking awesome. Besides I will protect you, baby," she said playfully tickling Sonya and kissing her on the cheek. Sonya agreed and got up to close the curtains before they turned the movie on.

Mia burst out into laughter at the way Sonya was acting and they hadn't even turned the movie on yet.

An hour had passed by, and they were both deep into the movie. They both jumped from being startled at the sound of the doorbell, dinging throughout the entire house. Sonya ran to the door after her heart stopped racing a little and grabbed the food from the delivery guy. She handed him a fifty dollar bill and shut the door in his face. She hopped back on the sofa with Mia, who had paused the movie, and waited for her to come back. After they sat the food down, Mia ran to get them some sodas and napkins for the greasy food products. They laughed at the parts that caused their hearts to jump out of their chests and enjoyed each other's company. After they finished watching The Conjuring, they watched part two right behind it.

Around one o'clock in the morning, they brought their festive evening to a finish. They cleaned up their mess and sent Lamar a text telling him 'goodnight' and that they loved him. Sonya was so scared to sleep so Mia held her closely and kissed her passionately, assuring her that she was there to protect her and that she was letting her imagination get the best of her. Even with Mia holding her in her arms, Sonya was still afraid to go to sleep; every little noise was frightening her. She eventually fell asleep almost two-thirty in the morning. She snuggled closer to Mia's warm body and drifted off to sleep, trying to block out the noises that crept through the night. It was damn near impossible.

Chapter Three
Baby Maker

"Did you hear that, Mia?" Sonya asked as she jumped up from out of her sleep. She looked over at the clock on the nightstand and saw that it was almost four o'clock in the morning. She heard another crash in the living room but was afraid to check it out. She shook Mia to wake her but she never got up.

"Leave me alone, babe, and go back to sleep. You're letting your imagination get the best of you like always," Mia replied grabbing Sonya around her waist again.

Sonya wasn't listening to that bullshit. She knew she heard something and she knew for damn sure that it wasn't all in her head. She slowly pulled the covers back and quietly eased out of the bed. She tiptoed out the room and into the hallway, careful not to step on any of the creaky spots. She peeped around the corner and squinted her eyes to see in the darkness and she knew for sure she saw a big figure rummaging through the closet. She took a deep breath and crept back into the room to try and wake up Mia again.

"Mia, Mia, wake up," she whispered into her ear as she shook her vigorously. Mia sat up saying 'what' through clenched teeth. Sonya immediately covered her mouth and whispered in her ear. "Listen. You hear that?"

"Oh shit. Somebody broke into the house?" Sonya nodded her head. Mia knew Sonya was scared by the way she was trembling in front of her. Mia hopped out the bed and handed Sonya her cell phone. "Take the phone and go down the hall to the guest bedroom and call the cops."

19

Trinity

"What the hell are you about to do?"

"Shit, I'm about to go see what the fuck is going on and see who the fuck is really that crazy to break into our damn house?"

"Be careful, baby?" Sonya said hugging Mia.

"You too, boo."

Sonya crept out the room and into the other bedroom, quickly dialing 911. She ducked down into the closet so she wouldn't be heard by the intruder. Mia, on the other hand, mind was set on protecting them and their house. Good thing Lamar taught them both how to shoot, but Sonya didn't like guns and tried to stay away from them as much as possible. She tiptoed over to the walk-in closet and pulled out the Mossberg 590 Shockwave 12 gauge pump. She heard footsteps heading into their bedroom and sat down in the closet, aiming the gun and getting ready. As soon as the person flicked their flashlight back on when they entered the closet, they gasped just before she pulled the trigger. They yelled out in agonizing pain as the bullet went through their shoulder, causing them to fly backwards onto the floor. Mia could hear Sonya scream and call her name as she ran down the hall. She flicked the light switch on and the room filled with light from the ceiling. Mia rose from the closet when she seen Sonya's pretty face emerge into the room.

"Oh my god, Mia, are you okay? Are you hurt?" Sonya asked frantically as she touched all over Mia looking for any signs of an attack.

"Boo I'm fine, okay? Did you call the cops?"

"Yes they should almost be here. Who the fuck is this?" Sonya asked kicking the masked perpetrator in the head and he yelled out in pain.

"I don't know, babe, but we about to find out." She handed Sonya the pump and she reluctantly took it and kept it aimed at the figure lying on their bedroom floor. Mia pulled the mask off the person's face and froze she couldn't believe who it was. They heard the police sirens and moments later they heard the cops walking throughout the house until they found them.

//

It was after 7 o'clock in the morning and the damn police were still there. Sonya and Mia had made coffee for the two officers that had showed up at the scene and arrested the scumbag. Now they were finally coming over to get their report out the way.

"So, ladies, first things first. We gave you all a chance to write down anything that was broken or stolen out the house. May I see your lists, please?" They both handed him their lists and he wrote down the items in his report. "Now, Ms. Jamison, did you know the intruder?"

"No, Officer, I didn't. I have never seen him before in my life," she responded.

"You answered that fairly quickly, Ma'am. You didn't even hesitate to answer the question," he replied as he wrote some more information down on his notepad.

"Well, what fucking reason would I have to wait to answer the question? If I don't know the little puta then I don't know the little puta. Shit!" she yelled.

"Ma'am calm down before I have to take you in."

"Fuck you, pig," she shot back as she got up and went to the bedroom.

"Anyway, Ms. Jacobs did you know who the intruder was? Have you ever seen him before around here?"

"Yeah, I know who he is but I don't know him know him. But, I know for sure that he doesn't live around here. He bumped into me at the mall earlier today. I don't think Sonya was really paying attention but I damn sure was."

"So, other than the mall, you have never seen him before?"

"Nope."

"That's kind of odd though."

"How so?"

"Out of all the women in the mall, he chose to come to your house and rob you two women. But yet you don't know this man from Adam and Eve," he said chuckling a little and shaking his head, continuing to write in his notepad.

"Maybe he was watching us the entire time in the mall but was being inconspicuous. Did you ever think about that?"

"What do you do for a living, Ms. Jacobs?" he asked not even acknowledging what she just did an entire rant about. Mia sucked her teeth and responded to his question.

"I'm a hairstylist," she said quickly.

"Damn, the hair business must be booming to afford a house out here. Wouldn't you say?"

"Look I don't know what the fuck you insinuating but you asking too many questions that ain't got a motherfucking thing to do with the fact that somebody just broke into our house," she replied as she rose to her feet and stood over top of the officer. He stood up and looked down at her 5'5" frame.

"Save that shit, lady," he replied through clenched teeth. "All you females are the same. You meet some rich guy and take advantage of him and do your best to stay in his good graces. I'm onto your game and if you ever want to step out, here's my card." He handed her his business card with his personal phone number etched onto it. They finished up and left the premises.

That motherfucker must think we're some whores or some shit Mia thought to herself. All she could do was laugh as she closed the door back and headed to the bedroom where she found Sonya rolling up a jay.

"Is that fucktard gone, baby?" Sonya asked as she blew a cloud of smoke into the air. Mia took the blunt from her and took a couple puffs before passing it back to her.

"Yeah, Mami. That dickhead had the nerve to tell me to call him if I ever want to step out on Lamar. I swear he must think this is a whorehouse and we got a pimp or some shit," she said. They both burst into laughter and continued to smoke the jay until it was all gone.

"I spoke to Lamar and he said he sending some people to the house to fix the locks and put in a better alarm system. He said he probably get a couple of dogs to keep outside too, but I told him that wasn't necessary."

"Exactly, he is doing the most."

"Yeah but he just protecting his girls."

"I know," Mia responded. They ended up falling back to sleep for a few hours. All of the excitement between last night and this morning were really taking a toll on them; they didn't even want to leave the bed that day. But they knew eventually they had to because they were supposed to be going to the grocery store.
Around 5 o'clock, the ladies woke up from their long, but much needed, nap. Sonya had heated up their pizza from the previous night and they watched reruns episodes of Snapped. As much as they loved sitting around lounging all day long, they knew they eventually had to get up and go do their dreadful errand of grocery shopping. After a while, they did a quick wipe down of their bodies and threw on a pair of jeans and some sneakers and headed to the BJ's.

23   Trinity

"It doesn't matter what time of day we come here, it's always packed and the lines be long as fuck for no reason," Mia said as she pushed the supersized shopping cart.

"Girl, I swear, you have never lied," Sonya replied as she grabbed another one of the oversized shopping carts.

Sonya and Mia had no worries in the world as they unconsciously threw items into the baskets. From bulks of cereal to bulks of bread and meat, the ladies were on a mission to stock up their household for at least until the next month. When they came upon the snack aisle, their eyes grew big and they started cheesing and grinning from ear to ear. Sonya grabbed a box of cinnamon graham crackers, some Nutri-grain fruit bars, and the variety box of Rice Krispies treats. Mia decided to switch up her snacks this month. She grabbed a box of plain Rice Krispies treats, some Teddy Grahams, and some Famous Amos cookies. They threw Lamar's snacks into the cart along with some drinks and bags of chips. Their last stop was the beauty section. They stocked up on deodorant, body wash, and toothpaste. Struggling to maneuver their heavy baskets, they eventually made their way to one of the short lines. After standing in line for all of five minutes, the cashier greeted them and started scanning the items in both carts. After everything had been rung up, the cashier totaled their groceries to $600. Mia handed the woman the cash with no problem and they headed out the store after receiving their receipt. They made their way to the car and packed everything in the trunk and the back seat as best as they could.

"You should have driven your car, too, Mia."

"I told you, Sonya. But no, you didn't want listen," she giggled.

"Ha, ha, ha. Next time don't listen to me."

"I'll make a note of that." Mia looked down at the time at on the radio and it was nearing seven. "We might as well pull into a drive-thru and grab something to eat."

"After spending all that money on all these groceries, you still want to eat take-out?"

"Hell yeah because who on earth about to be cooking? Not I, baby, no ma'am."

"I guess you're right," Sonya replied. They drove a little ways down the road and pulled into a Chick-Fil-A. As usual, the line was as long as the line is at the Department of Motor Vehicles. But you better believe they had several people walking through that drive-thru taking people's orders. *That's why I fucking love this place* Sonya thought to herself. After waiting only ten minutes to place their order, someone came up to their car and took their order and about ten or fifteen minutes later, they got their food. They were all smiles as they ate their food and headed home. Mia and Sonya pulled up to their house and noticed all the changes that had been made throughout their absence. There were security cameras, motion lights, and an alarm system that Lamar had sent them the code for.

"Oh my goodness," Mia exasperated.

"What's the matter, baby?" Sonya asked her as she stroked her hair.

"I'm freaking exhausted and I don't think neither one of us were thinking straight in the store.

"What you mean? Why you say that?"

"Bitch because, we have to carry all this shit in the house!" They broke into laughter and then took several trips back and forth taking all the boxes and packages of food into their house.

//

Later that night, Sonya snuck into the bathroom while Mia was relaxing and watching the news in the living room. She turned on the hot water and let it run until it filled the bottom of the Jacuzzi tub then she added some bubble bath. She left the bathroom and crept into the room to get her and Mia some toys to play with while they take their bath. She stripped out of her clothes and let them drop to the floor, before heading out to the living room. The news was going off as she entered the living room, and she tapped Mia's shoulder and whispered in her ear. "Would you like to join me, baby?" she asked licking Mia's ear. Mia turned to face her and she stood up and walked away. Mia's head whipped around and her eyes locked on Sonya's voluptuous ass. Her mouth started to water and she wanted to taste her boo. She turned off the TV and the lights and ran into the room, only to be stopped by Sonya at the entryway.

"Take off those clothes, baby," she instructed. Mia did as she was told and removed every article of clothing, then stood butt naked in front of Sonya. They grabbed each other's hand and Sonya led her to the bathroom where the bubble bath awaited them.

"What's all of this?" Mia asked. She looked around the bathroom and noticed all the candles that surrounded the Jacuzzi tub and the array of toys that was laid out on the steps that led into the tub. "What's all this?" she repeated.

"This is all for you, baby. I wanted to show you how much I love you and show you a good time."

"Oh really now?"

"Yep," Sonya replied as she took Mia by the hand and led her into the tub. She grabbed the pouf and began squeezing the warm soapy water over her back. She massaged her back for a while, helping her to relieve some of her tension and stress that had been built up in the past few days. She turned her around to face her, and buried her face in between her titties. She sucked on her nipples as she used her hands to massage and caress them. She kissed her lips and put her hand under the water, rubbing her fingers against her pussy. She pushed two fingers inside of Mia and caused Mia to throw her head back, moaning loudly throughout the bathroom. Her phone rung and she picked it up when she realized it was Lamar calling her on Facetime.

"Hey, Papi," Sonya responded when the phone connected. She was still playing with Mia's pussy when Lamar's face graced the screen.

"What are my babies doing?" he asked puffing on a cigarette.

"Oh, nothing. We just in here taking a nice bath," she said. She turned the camera on Mia who was breathing heavily.

"Hey, daddy," she said continuing to breathe heavily and talk through her moans. She came seconds later in the water.

"Ooh wee. It looks like I called just in time for the show."

"You definitely did, baby," Sonya said. "And there's more."

"Oh really?" Sonya nodded her head and picked up some nipple clamps and placed them on both her and Mia's nipples. She handed Mia one of the dildos and they both licked and sucked and shoved them down their throats, turning their boyfriend on as he watched. "Keep going, baby."

The two girls started kissing again and tonguing each other done. They both laid their heads back on the side of the Jacuzzi and stuck the dildos inside of their pussies, then pulling them out and sucking their juices off. They repeated this multiple times until all three lovers reached their climax.

"That was fucking amazing," Mia said as her breathing became normal again and she was coming down from her sexual high. She pulled Sonya into another passionate kiss and they focused in on the tiny cell phone screen at Lamar.

"I loved the show ladies. Glad I was a part of it," he smiled as he finished cleaning up his own mess.

"So glad that you joined us and enjoyed it, daddy," Sonya said seductively.

"No problem. Well, I'm about to jump in the sack and catch some sleep. I will give you two a call in the morning. I love y'all and good night."

"We love you, too, daddy," they said in unison. They blew him several kisses before he ended the Facetime call with them. They took turns washing each other's bodies before getting out of the Jacuzzi. They made it into the bedroom and oiled each other up before hopping in the bed themselves butterball naked.

/ /

"Why are you making this decision so damn hard?" Sonya asked Mia. They were in the store trying to figure out what to wear tonight for their ladies' night out.

"I don't know about you, Mami, but I gotta look good when I go out on the town."

"As do I but you see I found something to wear," Sonya replied holding up her outfit.

"Just give me fifteen more minutes," Mia begged as she continued to search the clothing racks in Forever 21.

Sonya rolled her eyes at Mia and walked out of the store, leaving her to figure this shit out for herself. *How hard is it to find something to wear to a fucking club?* Sonya thought to herself. She walked to the food court and saw their friends Alisha and Chanel. They were eating a salad and it looked so good, but she wasn't trying to eat right now. *Maybe I will pick up one to take home.*

"Is her ass still in that damn store?" Alisha asked Sonya as soon as she sat down. Sonya just smirked and nodded her head.

"That's ridiculous," Chanel chimed in. "Did you find what you were looking for though, Mamacita?"

"I surely did. I picked out a romper."

"Can we see it?" they asked in unison.

"Nope. You bitches can see it later," Sonya laughed at them.

"You fucking suck, Sonya," Alisha said stuffing a forkful of her salad into her mouth.

"That I do, but that's exactly why my boyfriend loves me," she smiled hard.

"Your girlfriend loves you for that, too," Mia said walking up to the table carrying three shopping bags.

"That is true also," Sonya said kissing Mia when she sat down. "Why the hell do you have three bags? You were supposed to only get one outfit for tonight. One."

"I know, I know, baby, but I couldn't help it. You know how I get when I go shopping."

"You right, I do know and that's why I hate shopping with your slow ass."

"Yeah, yeah, yeah," she replied playfully pinching Sonya's face.

"Can you two sluts cut that out," Chanel said and they all broke out into laughter. "So, what's the plan for tonight?"

"Well, I thought we should get a VIP table at Bliss and go there and shake our asses."

"Is that all you think about, Mia? Shaking your funky ass?" Alisha asked laughing.

"Bitch don't hate. You wish your ass was like mine, don't you?"

"Not at all. I don't want to be carrying all that luggage around."

"Bitch, please," she responded and they all laughed again. They finished conversing and went their separate ways. Sonya and Mia both grabbed a salad before heading to the parking garage to hop in their cars. Mia told Sonya she was going to be home in an hour or so. Sonya asked if she wanted her to go with her and she told her no because she had some errands to run. They kissed and parted ways until later. Mia waited in her car stalled pulling out of the parking garage and waited for Sonya to leave before dialing a number.

"Yeah, hello?" the deep baritone voice said on the other end of the phone.

"Hey, it's Mia, is everything set up for tonight?"

"It definitely is, baby girl. You know I got you."

"I know. You never disappoint me, boo."

"You got that right. I don't want any shit from you tonight like always."

"Boy ain't nobody going to be giving you no shit tonight. You know me."

"Exactly, I do know you, and that's why I said that." Mia ended the call and put her car in drive and exited the parking garage.

Mia arrived home almost two hours later, giving her only a little bit of time to eat her salad, and get dressed before the ladies arrived. Sonya was there already in the kitchen as always, getting her grub on.

"Hey, babe," Sonya said when she seen Mia.

"Hey, baby."

"Did you get done what you needed to do?"

"I surely did," she responded nonchalantly. As she moved around the kitchen, she didn't realize that Sonya's eyes were following her suspiciously. She caught her gaze when she turned back around after pulling a Gatorade from the fridge.

"So, what did you have to do?" she asked.

"Damn, what's with all the questioning?"

"I'm just asking, Mia. Why the fuck are you being so defensive?"

"Nobody's being defensive. I don't have to tell you every motherfucking thing that goes on in my life, Sonya," she yelled.

"Oh so it's like that now, Mia? We hiding secrets from one another and shit? That's cool with me. At least I know where the fuck we stand," she responded finishing up her food and throwing it into the garbage.

"Look, Sonya, it's not like that," Mia said softly as she reached for Sonya's hand. She snatched it away and went into one of the other bedrooms and slammed the door. Mia followed her and banged on the door but Sonya would not let up. She texted Mia from the other side of the door and told her that she would be fine and she would see her in a couple of hours when it was time for them to get ready. Mia sent her an apology text and told her she loved her. Reluctantly, she received one back seconds later.

/ /

Sonya finished putting on her eyeliner as she stood in the bathroom then stepped back to admire herself. As usual, her makeup and nude MAC lipstick was on point. She turned to face the full length mirror that hung on the back of the bathroom door and gawked at her reflection. The royal blue dress with the plunging neckline was hugging her curves nicely and exposing her breasts almost to the point where one of them could pop out, and expose her pierced nipples. Her sterling silver accessories and silver open-toe stilettos completed the ensemble to the tee. She ran her fingers through her hair and exited the bathroom after she was satisfied with her appearance. As she left the bathroom, she noticed that Chanel and Alisha was pulling up outside. She went over to the door and opened it for them. As they walked past her, giving her kisses on her cheek, she paid close attention to their outfits as well. Chanel was wearing sexy black cut out backless dress made by Giorgio Armani with a pair of red spiked heels. Alisha, having to be extra extravagant, had on an asymmetric textured-leather mini dress from the Alexander McQueen line. She completed her outfit with some black stilettos and a bracelet and choker set that matched her dress. Sonya gave both women their props and invited them into the kitchen for a drink, while they waited for her slow ass girlfriend.

"Why is it always your girlfriend that has to hold us up, Sonya?" Chanel asked as she drunk her Patron.

"Don't be coming for my baby, Chanel. I will take these heels off and fight you," Sonya laughed then took a shot of the Patron as well.

"Girl ain't nobody worried about your little ass. Just tell her to hurry up."

"What the hell are you in such a rush for?" Alisha asked Chanel, sipping on her Patron.

"Bitch because I'm ready to go and shake my ass that my mama gave me," she responded playfully twerking as she stood at the island.

"Okay, I'm ready ladies," Mia said as she emerged from the back. Sonya's mouth dropped open as she seen how good Mia looked in her all red romper. She had it zippered as far as it could go to cover her titties and her ass was practically falling out the bottom. She had on a pair of open-toed spiked heels as well and her jewelry she had purchased at the mall the other day.

"Wow, Mia. You look, wow," Sonya stuttered over her words.

"What? What's wrong, baby? I don't look good?" she asked in a panicking tone.

"No, no, no, you look great, baby," Sonya assured her. She walked over and tongue kissed Mia and her knees started to get weak and Sonya pulled away, catching her before she fell over.

"Can y'all chill with all that lesbian shit, please? We are ready to go," Alisha said grabbing her car keys and walking towards the door; Chanel following in tow.

"Are we all driving our cars?" Mia asked grabbing her clutch bag.

"It doesn't matter. We can ride together if you want," Sonya said.

"We can drive in separate cars. I have to fill my gas tank up anyway."

"Seriously, Mia?" Sonya asked.

"Yep," she said stealing a kiss from Sonya and grabbing her keys. They made sure their house was locked up and secured before they all pulled out the driveway and headed to the highway. They all had Dodge Chargers and were looking like they were part of an exclusive car club as they all raced down the beltway, heading to the club.

/ /

The music was bumping in the club and the four ladies were really feeling themselves. They had a free bottle of liquor at their VIP table and multiple guys were sending drinks over to them trying to win them over. Little did these guys know, the ladies appreciated the kind gestures, but they didn't want or need any of their asses. Sonya was sitting back on the sofa and enjoying the lap dance that Mia was giving to her. The bystanders were enjoying it as much as she was; some were even throwing money their way and kept pushing through the club.

"This is so much fun, baby," Mia said as she sat on Sonya's lap.

33

"I know, right?" she said back into her ear.

"I have to go to the bathroom, y'all," Alisha yelled over the music. They all grabbed their purses and held each other's hands as they made their way through the nightclub. As they bumped and maneuvered through the crowd, they were being pulled on, grinded on and grabbed by unknown hands. They had finally made their way to the other side of the club and breathed a sigh of relief upon entering the ladies' restroom.

"Those niggas are fucking pussy hungry out there," Chanel said laughing. She and Alisha went to use the bathroom, when two females came out of the stalls. Sonya and Mia laughed and frowned their faces up when the two women skipped the sink and went right back into the party.

"Those nasty ass bitches."

"They probably didn't even wipe their pussies after they finished peeing. They probably let that shit drip dry."

"They definitely did," Chanel called from the stall. "There isn't any tissue in here. Can somebody pass me some paper towels?" she asked. Mia and Sonya laughed and handed paper towels to both of their friends. After they finished, Sonya and Mia went to the bathroom as well. They all washed their hands and decided to take a couple of flicks in the big mirror on the wall.

"Oh shit, that's my song y'all," Alisha yelled as she dashed out the bathroom to the dance floor as soon as she heard Cardi B's new song "Money" start to blare through the speakers. The three friends dashed out and joined her on the dance floor, shaking and gyrating their asses.

They danced all over the dance floor as the liquor started to take over their bodies. The DJ went from Cardi B, to The Migos, to NBA Youngboy, to Go-Go classics. Mia and Sonya were dancing all up on one another while Alisha and Chanel were occupied by a sexy guy that was enjoying all that ass that was grinding on them. Two guys walked over to Sonya and Mia and observed them for a few moments before separating them from each other and rubbing up against them. Sonya was struggling to keep her dress from riding up over her ass cheeks, but Mia didn't have that problem tonight. The guys were trying to pull them further away from each other but the ladies weren't having that nonsense, not tonight. Chanel grabbed all of them by the hand and motioned back to the VIP section. They followed behind one another until they safely made it back to their table.

"Did y'all see how geeked those guys were to dance with us?" Alisha yelled over the music.

"Girl, yes. I think one dude had precum because his jeans got a little wet and that nigga didn't have a drink so that's the only possibility." The group of four burst into laughter and high fived each other. They threw back a couple more drinks and just sat around enjoying the atmosphere.

At almost closing time, a tall dark skinned guy came to their table. All the ladies looked at him like he was in the wrong place until he reached out and took Mia by the hand.

"Who the fuck is this, Mia?" Sonya asked standing up and grabbing Mia around her waist.

"Yo, chill, Sonya, it's not what you think."

"Then what the fuck is it?"

"Don't worry about it, damn," Mia responded walking past Sonya. Sonya glared at the guy that had his hand around her girlfriend's waist and smacking her ass cheeks. Sonya sat there fuming and turning red, on the verge of crying. Moments later, she had lost Mia in the sea of partygoers. She stood to her feet in search of her woman but didn't see her.

"I'm out of here, y'all," she said giving her friends a hug and kiss and grabbing her purse.

35   Trinity

"No, don't leave. We're all having fun," Alisha said trying to persuade her to stay.

"I came here to have fun with my girls and my girlfriend but it seems like she had other plans. I wonder if Lamar knows that she out here being sneaky and secretive." She was heading towards the door when she heard the DJ cut the music off.

"Ay, yo, yo, yo, what's up everybody? Is everybody having a good time?" An eruption of yells spread throughout the club from the crowd of people. "I got a friend here that has a special announcement for her girlfriend. Here you go, Ma."

"Hey, everybody, my name is Mia and I have a very special person in the crowd and I need her to come up to the stage with me."

Sonya paused when she saw and heard her girlfriend on the stage. She rolled her eyes and headed towards the stage. When she reached the stairs, the dude that pulled Mia away from their table held Sonya's hand as she made her way up the little stairs and then stood next to Mia. "What is going on, Mia?" she whispered in her ear. Mia didn't respond but continued on with her speech.

"This is my beautiful girlfriend, Sonya. Isn't she gorgeous, y'all?" There were claps and whistles surrounding them and then she continued. "Well, three years ago I met her when my boyfriend had brought her home. I know a lot of you are probably thinking 'what the fuck type of shit they got going on?' But, I will tell y'all its great being in a polygamist relationship. I get the best of both worlds and don't even have to cheat," Mia giggled. "Well, I wanted to show my boo how much I love her and appreciate her being here and putting up with my shit on top of our boyfriend shit." Mia reached into her back pocket and pulled out a small velvet box, and handed it to Sonya. Sonya's eyes bulged out of her head and she turned the box around, showing it to the patrons in the club. Mia had given her a platinum 2 karat Blue Nile solitaire pendant necklace. Sonya instantly broke down and shed happy tears as Mia removed the necklace from the box and placed it around her neck. The crowd was in an uproar as they embraced and kissed, tonguing one another down like they were in the privacy of their own home, instead of on display on the stage in a nightclub.

"Well that's what the fuck I'm talking about," the DJ said as he got the microphone back from Mia. "On that note, I'm glad y'all came out tonight, but it's time to get the fuck on. You ain't gotta go home but you gotta get the hell up outta here." Chanel and Alisha grabbed their things and rushed to the stage to hug their friends and to get a better glimpse of Sonya's new piece of jewelry. They were the last to leave the club as usual and they ended up getting a free round of drinks from the bartender. Sonya tipped her a one hundred dollar bill and told her they would see her next time. The only thing on her mind was getting home and fucking the shit out of Mia's ass.

The four ladies hopped in their cars as the valet had brought their cars to the front. Alisha headed to Hyattsville, Chanel headed to Capitol Heights, and Mia and Sonya headed to their home. They got there and noticed that Lamar's car was in the driveway. They were so excited to see him that they almost broke their necks getting into the house. They locked the door behind them and took their heels off, leaving them by the front door. They walked to the bedroom and Lamar was lying in the middle of the bed with nothing on but a pair of Calvin Klein boxers, covering up his already erect penis.

"Hey, ladies," he responded looking at them and licking his lips.

"Hey, baby," they said in unison.

"Y'all look scrumptious. Why don't y'all take those clothes off and come get in the bed with y'all man." The two women obliged and stripped down to nothing but a pair of skimpy panties. They climbed onto the bed, rubbing their bare skin against Lamar's.

"It's about that time, ladies," Lamar responded as he rubbed on their asses.

"What time is that?" Sonya asked licking his lips with her tongue while Mia kissed and sucked on his neck.

"It's time for us to make a baby." The lights went out and soft music began to play. Within the hour, all you heard were moans and sweet ecstasy drowning out the sound of Tank's song "When we."

Chapter Four
Five Months Later

The two women were busy throwing endless food into their shopping carts. They had grown so much in their pregnancies and they never seemed to be full. For Sonya, she had to have flaming hot Cheetos and nacho cheese dip for her cravings, while Mia kept it simple with pickles and vanilla ice cream. This was actually their third time coming to the store this week. Lamar had no complaints whatsoever. He had both of his beautiful girlfriends pregnant at the same time and he prayed to have both a girl and a boy. He didn't care which woman was giving birth to which, he was just excited. He was upset that he couldn't make their appointments because he had an empire to run, but they always gave him an update after their appointments. The ladies wobbled to the front of the store, making their way through the line, paying for their items and leaving the store in record time. They rushed back home and hopped on the couch, watching the Lifetime Movie Network, enjoying their snacks.

"Can you fucking believe this shit?" Mia asked Sonya breaking the silence while their movie went on a commercial break.

"Believe what shit? Are you talking about the movie?"

"No, baby. I'm talking about the fact that in four months we will be giving birth to our first babies."

"Yeah, I'm really excited," Sonya said with fake enthusiasm.

"Are you okay, Sonya?"

Trinity

"Me? Yeah, I'm great. It's just I'm a little nervous, you know? What if it hurts to deliver? What if I have to get a C-section? What if the ambulance doesn't make it out here in time before the baby comes?"

"Calm down, baby," Mia said grabbing Sonya by the hands and hugging her. Sonya hugged her back tightly and took a couple of deep breaths. "Everything is going to be okay. I got you, and so does Lamar, baby."

"I know," Sonya responded then pulled away from Mia.

"If it makes you feel any better, I'm a little nervous, too."

"Really?"

"Mm-hmm, but I know I got you two."

"You surely do, babe." The girls gave one another a kiss and got back to their movie marathon. The cordless phone rang and Sonya volunteered to go and answer it so Mia could continue to relax.

"Hello?" she said as soon as she snatched the phone from the wall.

"Yes, this is Dr. Alawishus Montgomery, and I am calling for Mia James. Is she available?"

"Yes, she is, hold on one sec," Sonya replied. She walked over and handed the phone to Mia. She decided to take this time to go to the bathroom for the umpteenth time in the past three hours. When she finished, she joined Mia back into the living. She was sitting back down on the couch just as Mia ended her phone call. "Is everything okay, Mia?"

"It's better than okay. That was my doctor telling me that my sonogram had come back."

"So? What are we having?"

"Well, I wanted to wait until Lamar was here, but I guess I can tell him later. I'm having a little boy," she yelled excitedly.

"Oh my god that's great news. I'm so happy for you," Sonya said hugging her.

"You don't know what you're having yet?"

"Not yet. I have an appointment next week so I hope I find out then."

"I hope your ass have a little boy. That way Lamar can have both his son and daughter, and we won't have to get pregnant anymore," Mia said laughing.

"You right about that. I hate not being able to see my feet."

"Boo, that should be the least of your worries. You see my feet? My feet look like pig's feet, and that's on the real," she said holding her feet up as far as she could from the ground. Her feet had swollen tremendously and the majority of the time, she couldn't even wear sneakers for a long period of time. They both laughed and giggled together, then Sonya instructed Mia to place her feet into her lap so she could rub them. "Wow, that feels so good, baby," Mia responded leaning her head against one of the oversized couch cushions.

"I'm glad you're enjoying it, baby." Sonya rubbed her feet a little while longer, until Mia had dozed off into a deep slumber. As soon as Mia had fallen asleep, Sonya took this opportunity to go in the room and take a nap. Her back was killing her and that Serta memory foam mattress was calling her name. As soon as she laid down, she heard the doorbell ring. "Why me?" she whined. She started not to move but they kept ringing the damn doorbell, and Mia's ass was deaf as hell when she was sleeping. One would think she was either dead or in a coma because she didn't hear shit or move at all for that matter. Sonya took a deep breath as she passed Mia on the couch, and made her way to the door.

"How are you doing today, ma'am?" a FedEx worker replied. Sonya's face said it all and he continued. "I have a delivery for you," he responded as he grabbed the dolly and pushed it into the house when Sonya gave him the 'okay' to enter their home.

"What the hell is it?" she asked as she looked at them tall box.

"Ma'am, I don't know. I just deliver the items that are put on my truck. Can you sign here, please?" he asked her as he handed her the handheld to put her name on the line. She handed it back to him and pushed him out of the house so she could get some sleep. She made it back to the room and decided to give Lamar a call.

"Hey, baby, what's up?" he replied when he answered the phone. Sonya could hear the echo and knew who was using the speakerphone in the car.

"Hey, babe, you just got a package delivered from FedEx. Do you want me to open it?"

"You are so damn nosey," he said laughing into the phone. "Don't open it yet, Sonya. I want you both to open the box together. Where is Mia?"

"Taking her afternoon nap as usual," she snapped a little. The phone went silent for a few seconds. "Babe? Are you still there?"

"Yeah, I'm still here. I had to remember you were pregnant for a second the way you just snapped at me. It must be your hormones. I think you better go take a nap as well, Sonya."

"I would, but between the phone ringing off the hook and the doorbell consistently ringing, a girl can't sleep," she ranted.

"Look, Mami, I love you and I need you to get some rest. The baby needs rest," he said softly. She blew a kiss through the phone and ended the call. She looked at the box one more time, wondering what was inside of it, before heading back into the room. She climbed onto the bed and lay as

42   Trinity

comfortable as she possibly could with a couple of pillows secured behind her back, and drifted off to sleep.

Hours had passed by, and Mia was up stuffing her face with marshmallows and hot Cheetos. Sonya stretched in the bed and got up feeling a lot better. She went to the bathroom to pee and get herself together, before heading to the kitchen. She went over to Mia and kissed her on the neck.

"Hey sleepy head," Mia exclaimed giving Sonya a peck on her lips. She scooted over at the island and made room for Sonya. Sonya went to the fridge to grab her jar of pickles and vanilla ice cream. She dumped some of the hot Cheetos and marshmallows on top and dug in. "Hey is that good?"

"It definitely is," Sonya replied. She got back up to retrieve a spoon for Mia and handed it to her. They both took turns dumping hot Cheetos and marshmallows into the small ice cream container; eating until it was completely finished.

"That was so good and it really hit the spot."

"It definitely made me feel better," Sonya replied. "Girl, why you didn't wake me up when you woke up?"

"You were sleeping so peaceful and I didn't want to disturb you, baby. By the way, what's in that box over there?" Mia asked pointing to the spot where the FedEx driver left the package.

"Beats me, babe. I called Lamar about it and he said he wanted you and me to open it together."

"Well what the hell are we waiting for? Let's open that sucker," Mia replied happily as she hopped down from the stool and wobbled over to the box.

"Vamos chica," Sonya replied as she followed behind Mia. They both grabbed a box cutter from the drawer of one of the end tables and cut through the packaging. They eyes became filled with joy when the items fell out of the box. They picked the boxes up and examined them as they sat them on their laps.

"Aww, this is so sweet," Mia replied starting to get emotional already.

"It is," Sonya cried along with her.

Lamar had gotten both babies a jungle themed bouncer seat and some books for the women to read to them. Sonya picked up another smaller box that had fallen out of the bigger box and opened it with Mia. Inside were two $500 gift cards for them to use at Burlington Coat Factory to shop for the babies. They both held each other and cried hysterically. Sonya pulled out her cell phone and called Lamar's phone, putting it on speakerphone. Unfortunately he didn't answer the phone and they ended up shooting him a text message.

"This was really nice of Lamar to do. That's why I love that boy," Mia said softly, wiping her tears away.

"Yeah, I love his chocolate ass, too, girl," Sonya replied wiping away her tears as well. "We should do something for him, Mia."

"I think we should, too. What did you have in mind?"

"Maybe we should take him to a nice restaurant or something," Sonya suggested.

Mia pondered the thought for a minute or so before continuing. "That's a good idea, but we're always going out. We should cook him a really nice dinner here. We can run to Bath & Body Works and grab some nice scented candles and have a candlelit dinner. How does that sound?"

"Oh, you trying to be romantic huh?" they both giggled and ended up deciding to do that.

"Great! I'm gonna go hop in the shower and get ready. It's already four o'clock and he will probably be here about nine. We can run to the store and grab the stuff and hurry back here."

"Cool with me, babe. I will hop in the shower down the hall and get ready," Sonya said starting to walk away. Mia gently pulled her back by her pajama shirt. "What's wrong?"

"What's wrong? So you don't wanna take a shower with me, baby?" Mia asked rubbing on Sonya's big stomach.

"I wish I could join you but both of our big ass stomachs are not gonna fit in that damn shower, babe," Sonya said laughing.

"You right, you right. I'm gonna let you have that one." Mia kissed her girlfriend and they went their separate ways to get ready.

/ /

The two women had made it back home by six o'clock, with ample time to get everything ready. They would have been finished but they went crazy in Bath & Body Works. The store had an outstanding end of the summer sale on everything in the store. Instead of getting just candles for tonight, Sonya and Mia had gone bananas buying up endless lotions, perfumes, and fragrances for both their cars and their home. While Sonya was steaming the lobster in the big pot, Mia was searing their steaks and a big, juicy, T-bone steak for Lamar. The house was filled with the sounds of Lauryn Hill, and smelled of vanilla and a delicious meal as Lamar walked into the house unnoticed.

"Hey, ladies, what's up?" he asked walking in carrying two bouquets of multicolored roses. The two women damn near jumped out of their skin when he startled them.

"Babe, what are you doing home so early?" Sonya asked walking over to him.

"Right, baby, you ruined our surprise for you," Mia responded with a sad face as she walked over to Lamar as well. They both gave him a kiss on his lips and he handed them each a bouquet of roses.

"It's okay, ladies, I am still surprised. This is a nice surprise and it smells good in here," he replied walking past them and walking over to the stove. "Wow, lobster and steak for dinner?"

"Yep and baked potatoes with sour cream," Sonya added. He went to each woman, passionately kissing them both before he thanked them for their generosity, and went to take a hot shower.

By the time he had gotten out of the shower a half hour later, the table was already set and the unscented stick candles were placed in the middle of the table in the crystal candle stick holders. Lamar went to the room and threw on a pair of pajama bottoms and came back to the table shirtless. The two ladies gawked over their boyfriend's chiseled body that he earned while in prison. His abs was so nice and tight you could use them as a washboard. Their names were tattooed on his chest right over his heart, and they had his name tatted in the same spot. He sat down and joined them at the table, and the threesome enjoyed their delicious meal with a glass of Chardonnay.

"Dinner was great, ladies," Lamar said to Mia and Sonya as soon he wiped his mouth and finished off his wine.

"Thank you, love," Mia responded kissing his lips and taking his champagne flute and plate. Sonya followed and picked up the remaining dishes on the table.

"We're glad you enjoyed it, Papi," she said with her deep Spanish accent. As the two women washed and dried the dishes together, Lamar just sat back in the chair observing their asses and protruding bellies. Since being pregnant, they both had put on some pounds but they were all going to the right places. Their breasts were getting fuller and their pretty faces were getting a little fatter, it didn't bother him though. He liked how the pregnancies enhanced their beauty and gave them a glow. He only had four more months to go before he was welcoming his babies. Mia told him over dinner that they were having a little boy but he still didn't know what Sonya was having. She told him that she would find out next week and he wanted to go but she told him he didn't have to. He thought that was kind of odd but he didn't let it deter him and disturb their dinner. After the ladies finished the dishes, they all went to the room to get ready for bed.

"You wanna take a shower with us?" Mia asked Sonya as she turned on the shower water before stepping back into the room to get their pajamas.

"No that's okay, baby. I think I'm coming down with a cold or something. So I think I will just take a shower in the other bathroom and sleep in one of the other rooms. I don't want to get Lamar sick and I especially don't want you and your baby getting sick."

Lamar and Mia both looked at one another suspiciously then looked back at Sonya. "Okay, sweetie, we understand," Mia responded. She gave Sonya a kiss on her cheek and told her that she hoped she felt better in the morning. Sonya walked over to Lamar and he gave her a kiss on her other cheek. She grabbed a towel and washcloth, along with some pajamas and headed down the hall to the other bathroom.

After they all finished their showers, Sonya went to sleep in the room directly next to the master bedroom. Mia and Lamar were up talking for hours, and Sonya didn't miss a beat as she listened in.

"Do you think Sonya is okay, L?" Mia asked as she lay in Lamar's arms, rubbing her fingertips across his bare chest.

"What do you mean, babe? Did she say something?"

"No she didn't but I'm just saying. It seems like she's been acting different since we got pregnant five months ago. She's been kind of distant and standoffish or something."

"I'm not sure what you mean, Mia. I haven't noticed any change really in neither one of y'all except the fact that y'all been packing away the snacks," he said jokingly.

"Stop playing with me," she responded playfully punching him in the midsection. "Maybe I'm just overreacting or something."

"Maybe the pregnancy is just getting to her, that's all. Stop worrying so much about nothing, baby girl."

"Maybe we should go and hangout tomorrow. You know, have a girl's day out or something."

"That sounds cool. I will leave the American Express card here for y'all to do y'all thing."

"You're so good to us," Mia said kissing him on the lips.

"How good is daddy to you and Sonya, baby?" he asked between kisses.

"I'll show you," she responded as she climbed on top of him, careful not to lean in too much that she would hurt the baby.

The room filled with ecstasy and was heard in Sonya's room. With each moment passing, she shed a tear wishing that she was in there with them, enjoying their lovemaking session. *Maybe I will feel better tomorrow* she thought to herself.

///

Over the past week, Sonya have been having mixed emotions about her relationship with Lamar and Mia. It seemed like they were spending more time together than she and Lamar was. The day after she wasn't feeling well, she and Mia had spent a few hours out the house. They walked around the mall shopping and getting their exercise in for the day. They even went to get their nails and feet done to enjoy some relaxation. But after that day, every little thing Mia did would annoy Sonya. It wasn't even serious stuff but dumb shit. For example, she had just spazzed on Mia two days ago for sitting in her spot on the couch. It's not like it was a big deal as she thought about it now, but at the moment she was pissed. She had yelled at Mia so harshly that it had driven her to tears. She had called Lamar crying and he fussed at Sonya about her behavior. He told her that she had better stop stressing Mia out and getting riled up before they both ended up losing their babies or cause them to go into an early labor. Sonya apologized but she didn't really mean it. She felt as though they were both in cahoots with one another and ganging up on her. And it would make a little sense because Sonya was welcomed into their relationship, and Mia was there first, but she didn't read too much into that thought. Maybe it's just the pregnancy that has me tripping and shit she thought. But she brushed all her thoughts to the back of her mind because today was the day that she would find out what she was carrying in her belly all of this time. And nothing or nobody was going to stand in the way of her excitement; nope not today.

Sonya got up again this morning, without neither one of her partners next to her. She checked her phone and she didn't even have any missed calls or text messages from them. She tried calling Lamar but he didn't answer the phone; probably because he was at work. She ended the call and dialed Mia's number; she picked up right before the phone went to voicemail.

"Good morning, sunshine," Mia sang cheerfully into the phone when she answered.

"Hey, baby, where are you?" Sonya asked as she brushed her teeth.

"I'm just leaving the post office. I had to send a letter to my mom up in New York. What are you doing?"

"I'm in the house getting ready for my doctor's appointment."

"Oh goody do you mind if I go with you?"

"No it's okay. I'm just going to get my sonogram done and then coming back home." The phone became silent on Mia's end. After a few seconds of uneasiness on the phone, Sonya continued to talk. "I would love for you to come but I just want surprise you and Lamar like you did us."

"I totally understand, babe. Well I guess I will see you when you get back home. I love you, Sonya."

"I love you, too, Mia," Sonya responded before hanging up the phone. She hurried and threw on a pair of her maternity leggings and a t-shirt. She grabbed her oversized purse and her phone and headed out the door to Southern Maryland Hospital Center. As she was hopping in her car, she had seen the mailman. They waved at one another and she left.

Sonya had arrived at her appointment on time and then after waiting about fifteen or twenty minutes, the nurse had come out and called her to the back. She walked past several rooms where other moms were in there for appointments, some way bigger than she and Mia was. She made it to her room and the nurse went over her vitals and made sure everything was good with her. Once everything was confirmed, she told her to just relax and the doctor would be in momentarily. As soon as the nurse left the room, Sonya hopped down with her purse in hand and started searching through the cabinets and drawers. Just like any other time, she stuffed her purse with bandages, gauze, tape, and a couple of boxes of tissues. She heard a light knock at the door and hurried back to the chair. As soon as she sat down the door opened and in walked Dr. Mabel Johansen with a big smile spread across her face.

"So how are we doing today Ms. Jamison?"

"Oh I'm doing good doc. I'm just excited to find out if I'm having a boy or a girl."

"So am I," she responded as she rubbed her hands with sanitizer before placing a pair of latex gloves over her hands. "Do you mind pulling your pants down a little and covering up with this?" she said handing her one of the paper blankets from the drawer. Sonya did as she was told and prepared for her ultrasound. After a while, and many clicks and typing later, the results for the sex of the baby were complete. The doctor looked to Sonya with a bright smile, and told her what she was being blessed with. Sonya was so ecstatic that she almost cried. Not tears of pain but tears of joy.

/ /

"So what did they say, baby?" Mia asked Sonya as soon as she walked into the house.

"Damn can I get in the house first, chica?" Sonya asked laughing. She sat her purse down beside her as she flopped down on the sofa next to Mia. Mia leaned in and gave her a kiss and rubbed and kissed on her belly. Seeing the way Mia was reacting was bringing a smile to Sonya's face and she couldn't hold back the news anymore. She pulled the folded sonograms out of her bag and handed them to Mia.

"Yay you got the ultrasound done! I can't wait to see them."

"Where is Lamar?" Sonya asked peeping in the back to see if he was lying down in the bed.

"Oh he's still at work did you wanna call him before you gave me the news?"

"Yeah I kind of did," she said nervously.

"No problem, let's call him," Mia said as she pulled out her phone and called Lamar on Facetime. He answered in two rings. "Hey, baby," she said.

"Hey baby girl, what's up?"

"Nothing much. Sonya's back from her appointment and she brought us sonograms," she said waving the papers in front of the phone and putting Sonya on the video chat.

"How you feeling, baby?" Lamar asked Sonya.

"I'm good just a little nervous. I just hope you two will be as excited as I am about the baby."

"We will be," both Mia and Lamar said simultaneously. Mia handed the folded up papers back to Sonya, who slowly unfolded them and exposed the truth.

"Twins?!" They both said together.

"Yes twins! I'm having a boy and a girl!"

"This is so great!" Mia said dropping the phone onto the couch and squeezing Sonya tightly in her arms.

"Hey, hey, hey can I get some love too?" Lamar said from the phone. The girls picked the phone up and apologized to their boyfriend and then ended the call with him.

The girls continued to hug again and then went on to planning their baby shower. They picked out the decorations for the baby shower, the theme, and even the invitations. They decided to do a PJ Masks theme and do a list for who was going to be the godparents and who they were going to invite to the function in general. After the list was completed, they each did a baby registry and loaded their lists up with stuff that they either wanted or needed for their babies from both Babies 'R' Us and Burlington. This went on for hours until they got everything in order and had stuffed their bellies with endless food and snacks, then before you knew it, they were both asleep on the couch by the time the clock struck ten.

Chapter Five

Three Months Later

It had been a long past three months for the two women and Lamar. Both Mia and Sonya had looked to be gaining weight nonstop and Lamar loved every minute of it. Today was the day that all have been waiting for; the baby shower. Alisha and Chanel had come over the past couple of nights to help their friends set up for the shower and last night they put the final touches on the decorations. Sonya checked the time and saw that it was almost one o'clock and they had to get out the house and pick up the food and cake from the caterers. Just as she was getting ready to knock on the bathroom door again, the door had flown open and Mia wobbled out.

"It's about time you brought your ass out the bathroom."

"Don't start it, Bae. I'm really cranky this morning."

"What's the matter, sweetie?" Sonya asked stroking Mia's hair and caressing her shoulders.

"I'm just nervous. Any day now, we will be delivering these children and I don't think I'm ready. What if I'm no good at being a mother?"

"Girl hush with all that damn negativity. You will be a great mother and so will I. You have nothing to worry about, Mia. We're a team and the kids will have the best dad and mothers. I promise you," she replied. She brought Mia's face to hers and kissed gently kissed her soft lips.

"Thank you, baby, I really needed that pep talk."

"That's what I'm here for. Well that and great sex."

"You are definitely not lying about that," they both laughed together. The two ladies grabbed their purses and headed out of the house, headed to Mia's car.

"So where are we headed to first, boo?" Mia asked as she adjusted her seat before starting the car.

"I guess to get the food and snacks. Then we can go and get the cake from Costco."

"I just hope these stores aren't packed like they always are, Sonya."

"Do you realize that every time we say that the places are always packed? Besides it's going to be packed anyway because Thanksgiving is next week."

"Oh shit I forgot about Thanksgiving," Mia replied as she drove out the driveway and down the street, riding through the suburban streets.

"I know right? I am not ready to deal with my mother and my father," Sonya replied blowing air out of her mouth.

"Girl who you telling? My mother and stepfather and no damn cakewalk either. But luckily it's only for one day and after that we don't have to see their asses until Christmas."

"Maybe not even then because our fat asses might be in the hospital."

"I hope and pray that we are," Mia laughed and Sonya joined in. The couple drove a little more before arriving at the Costco in Woodmore Town Center. They decided to split up when they got in the store to make the trip quicker than ever. Mia grabbed a shopping cart and headed to grab the snacks and Sonya grabbed another shopping cart and headed to the bakery to get the cake for the baby shower.

"How are you doing, Ma'am?" Sonya said as she approached the bakery.

"How are you doing?" the older lady responded coming closer to where Sonya was. "Oh my, my, my, you look like you're ready to drop any day now," she replied laughing gingerly.

"I wish," Sonya smiled. "They're not due until Christmas Day."

"They? You mean more than one?"

"Yes, Ma'am. I'm having twins."

"Congratulations, sweetheart. Now what can I help you with?"

"I'm here to pick up the baby shower cake for Sonya Jamison."

"Okay give me a minute." The lady disappeared behind a set of double doors. Sonya walked away momentarily and observed all of the delicious looking donuts and Danishes that were setup nicely on the table. She grabbed a container of glazed donuts and tossed them in the cart; she and Mia could eat those on the way home. She saw the lady come back and walked back over as the lady came from behind the counter. As she placed the large cake in the cart, Sonya smiled.

"Wow it looks amazing."

"Well thank you, sweetheart. I try my best."

"This is exceptional work," Sonya said as she looked at the detail on the cake. There were doves and a stork on top of the cake. The borders were both baby blue and pink with her and Mia's names on it. She almost cried but held the tears back. She thanked the lady and headed to the end of one of the long ass lines.

"What chips should I get?" Mia thought out loud. She scanned the variety bags of chips and decided on Tostito's and Doritos and some pretzels. She threw in two bags of each and some salsa and cheese dips. She thought about picking up some drinks as well but L would cuss her out if she lifted that heavy stuff so she decided against it. She did however grab a big thing of chocolate turtles and popcorn for her and Sonya. Shit, after all they had been dealing with lately they deserved it; at least that's what she thought. She smiled to herself as she made her way up to the line where she saw her girlfriend standing.

"Did you get everything, sweetie?" Sonya asked as soon as Mia walked up to her.

"I think so, baby," Mia replied as she and Sonya both scanned the contents of the basket. Mia looked at the cake lying in Sonya's cart and smiled.

"Do you know that I love you, Mia?" Sonya randomly said as they moved up a little in the line.

"Yes I know that, but why did you ask?"

"No reason, baby. I was just reassuring you," she said.

"Aww you're gonna make me cry, Mami. I love you, too, babe," Mia said kissing Sonya's lips. When they parted lips, they were welcomed with a disgusted look from an older woman standing behind them.

"Damn can we have our faces back?" Sonya yelled at the lady.

"Excuse me? Who are you talking too!?"

"Obviously you, Aunt Jemima. Why you all up in our faces and minding our business?"

"You two ought to be ashamed of yourselves. Sinners. And then you both have the nerve to be pregnant. Jesus Lord help these young folk. Have mercy on their souls."

"You're about to feel some damn mercy if you don't leave my goddamn girlfriend alone," Mia replied jumping in and coming to Sonya's rescue. She started toward the woman but the woman grabbed ahold of her shopping cart and hurried away from the women.

"Don't worry about Ms. Muriel," the cashier said as they approached her. "She's always in here and always stirring up trouble. You two are a beautiful couple and congratulations."

"Thank you," they both said in unison. They paid for their items and hurried to Mia's car, noticing that it was almost three o'clock and the baby shower was set to start at 4 o'clock. Mia sped down the highway to their home, making it home fifteen minutes earlier than usual. When they arrived to the house, they saw Lamar's car and beeped the horn repeatedly until he emerged from the house.

"Hey, babies, did you miss me?" he asked grinning from ear to ear as he approached the car.

"Of course we did. You and those big strong muscles of yours," Mia said jokingly squeezing his biceps.

"Oh yeah? Why do I have this strange feeling that you two are up to something?"

"Because we always are. Can you help us with all of this heavy stuff, L?" Sonya asked in her soft voice as she walked to the other side of the car, stroking his goatee.

"You know I can't say no to those eyes, baby," he replied licking his lips. He leaned in for a kiss and Sonya moved back and grabbed Mia by the hand.

"Sorry babe we gotta go and get ready for our baby shower," Mia said. They hurried into the house to get ready while L just laughed at them and began to unload the car.

"This party is turning out great," Chanel said. The crew looked around at all of the attendees and enjoyed the scene. It had only been going on for two hours but so many people had shown up within the first hour. Now, everybody were mingling, snacking, or dancing to the music that bumped through the speakers of the Bose stereo.

"Si, Mami, it definitely is. It's better than I expected," Sonya said smiling.

"I didn't expect so many people to show up honestly but I'm glad they did," Mia said in agreement.

Lamar walked away from his friends and walked over to the table where his queens were sitting on their thrones that he bought them. "If I haven't told you two yet today, you both look great and I cannot wait to tear y'all asses up later," he whispered making both of them blush and giggle like two teenage school girls.

"You three need to get a room," Alisha said walking back over to the table where her friends were.

"How did you even hear what I said when you didn't even hear what I said?" Lamar asked.

"Didn't have to. I know how to read lips," she said winking at Lamar. The four women laughed.

"See y'all nosey as hell," he said. He kissed his girlfriends on their cheeks and told them he would bring them some fruit back.

"I wasn't all for y'all relationship at first but I'm glad y'all got blessed with a good and fine man like that," Chanel said.

"We are kind of lucky aren't we, Sonya?"

"Si, Mami. We couldn't have been luckier; even when it comes to you and me." She leaned over to kiss a blushing Mia and they were unaware of the audience that had all eyes on them until they heard all of the clapping. They both giggled and smiled at one another, looking at each other the only way lovers looked at one another.

As the party went on later into the evening, the attendees were getting wasted from the unlimited alcohol provided by Lamar and his boys. They opened all of their gifts and literally received everything that they had asked for. They were happy because that was going to save them some much needed money for their children. Around 8 o'clock, they had lost most of their guests but only Chanel and Alisha stayed to help clean up. Lamar and his friends were even helping but I think the guys stayed only to hang with my girls, which was fine with me and Sonya, as long as they helped. They heard the doorbell ring and I went to go see who had been this much of a late arrival to our little shindig. The smile dropped from my face when I swung open the door and realized that it was my mother and stepfather.

"Mom? Joseph? What are you two doing here?" I asked in astonishment.

"Is that any way to talk to your mother Mia? Let us in," she demanded. Before I could even move out the way good enough, they both rushed through the front door. She came in looking around as he sat down a suitcase.

"Nice place you got here, Mia," her stepfather Joseph replied hugging her.

"I see that thug done finally knocked you up, but I don't see a damn ring," her mother stated. *Here we go* Mia thought to herself.

"Don't start, Mom, I am so not in the mood for your crap tonight."

"You watch your mouth young lady. You will not speak to your mother like that. Especially while I'm here."

"And you will not disrespect my woman while I'm here," Lamar said walking up to the door where they all were.

"Hello, Lamar," Mia's mother replied and rolled her eyes.

"How are you doing, Ms. Tonya. Mr. Joseph, how are you?" he asked looking his way. Joseph shook his hand and dropped it instantly.

"Well, Lamar, I see you have completely brainwashed my daughter and got her pregnant. So what are your plans now? Do you plan on marrying her?" she asked with her hands on her chubby hips.

"Well I mean we haven't discussed anything yet. So if and when we do decide, you will be the first to know," he responded sarcastically then walked away.

"Hey everyone," Sonya said peeping her head into the living room at the commotion.

"Mom, Joseph there is somebody I would like for y'all to meet," Mia said waving Sonya over to join them. "This is our girlfriend, Sonya. Sonya this is my mother, Tonya and my stepfather, Joseph."

"It's nice to meet you both," Sonya replied respectfully. Joseph shook her hand gently but Tonya smacked her hand away in disgust.

"Our? Girlfriend? What the fuck is going on here, Mia?!" she yelled.

"Don't yell in our house please. You'll upset the babies."

"Babies? And both of y'all are pregnant? This is fucking insane."

"Look, Ma'am, I don't know what's going on but I think I'm gonna just leave. Babe, I'm gonna go help finish cleaning up. Do you need anything?"

"Nothing, baby, thank you though." The two women locked lips and both Joseph and Tonya's mouths dropped. Joseph thought it was hot even though that was his stepdaughter, but Tonya on the other hand looked like she was about to snatch Sonya up by her long hair.

"Really, Mia, you're dating a woman now?"

"We're dating a woman, ma. I just said Sonya was both me and Lamar's girlfriend."

"Good Lord. How long has this been going on?"

"For about three years now."

"Are they making you do this, sweetheart? Do they have you on drugs or something? Are they holding you here against your will? If so you can tell me and your father, dear."

Mia looked dead in her mother's eyes and burst into uncontrollable laughter. "No, ma'am, it's not any of those things at all. I am here willingly and I love the both of them. And for the umpteenth time he is not my father," she said glaring at Joseph who stood there silently.

"How could you love two people at the same time? And one of those people is a goddamn woman!"

"I'm not about to stand here and let you keep disrespecting my man and my woman. Skipping the subject, what are you two doing here anyway, ma?"

"Didn't you invite us down here for Thanksgiving?" she responded with a deep exhale.

"But Thanksgiving isn't until Wednesday and its Saturday."

"Well if I would have known about this crazy circus going on in here I would have waited to come or wouldn't have come at all."

"You should have called first," Mia said rolling her eyes and sucking her teeth.

"I wanted to surprise you but it seems like I'm the one that got surprised. The Lord did not have this in his plan. Its man and woman, Mia. Not man, woman, woman. What on earth is wrong with you? I raised you better than that."

"Look, you and Joseph either accept it or not. If you accept it, we are more than happy to welcome the two of you to our home. If you disagree, well there's the door. This conversation is over," Mia responded as she wobbled away and went into the den to join the others. Her mother and Joseph just continued to stand there looking dumbfounded.

"Is everything okay, Mia?" Chanel asked as she approached Mia once she entered the den. She saw a tear fall from Mia's eye and roll down her cheek upon closer inspection. She rushed to Mia and threw her arms around her. When Sonya and Alisha saw how torn up Mia looked, they rushed to her aide as well. The four woman stood there holding one another. Lamar was standing across the room observing his girls and their friends.

"Baby don't worry about that shit. They just don't understand what's going on," Sonya said consoling her girlfriend. Alisha and Chanel made room when they saw L walking over towards them.

"Sonya is right, Mia. Don't let that bullshit from your mother and Joseph put a damper on y'all day. Hell don't let it get you down at all. You know I love both you and Sonya and my kids that y'all will be blessing me with soon," he said dropping to his knees and rubbing both of their bellies and kissing them.

"I guess you guys are right," Mia said wiping her face. She gave both L and Sonya a kiss then continued to help clean up the rest of the mess. Within an hour, they were all finished and ready to go to bed for the night. When Mia and Sonya walked Chanel and Alisha to the door, Mia saw that her parents were still there; sitting comfortably in the living room and watching television. Mia briskly walked past and out the front door. The four ladies spoke for a few minutes before hugging and parting ways. Sonya and Mia walked back in and locked their door. They were walking past the sofa when Mia's mother stopped the two.

"Look Sonya and Mia I apologize for how I acted earlier this evening. It's just Mia should have told me what was going on. I didn't even know my own child was into women let alone this kind of craziness. I mean when it's y'all time to die hopefully God opens the gates and let you in but live your life how you want I guess. But did you all think about the children and how they will feel in this situation?"

"Yes we have thought about it, mother," Mia lied. "And what the hell kind of apology is that?"

"I'm so out of here, Mami," Sonya said to Mia. "Good night Mr. and Mrs. Goodman." She walked to their room and laid down with Lamar.

"Its okay, Mia, if you pray and confess your sins. You may still have a chance if you repent and leave this situation alone."

"If you don't cut the shit you will have to leave. Leave this house, leave this state, and leave my life. I will not say another word about this. If you two want to stay, you know where the guest room is." Mia walked away from her mother and stepfather once again. She turned back around briefly to her mother. "By the way there's a lot about me you don't know, Ma. Good night," she said. Her mother went to sit back down with her husband when Mia disappeared into her room and closed the door.

"Why don't you just leave that damn girl alone, Tonya," Joseph said facing his wife.

"Are you really gonna sit there and tell me you are siding with them? You're condoning this shit, Joseph Goodman?" she yelled at him.

"She looks happy, they all do. Who the hell are we to come in and try to disrupt their happy home?"

"Happy home, Joseph, really? This is ungodly and my daughter will be punished for her sins and so will those other two."

"Well let them deal with that when their time comes. Stop nagging so damn much."

"Nagging! You call the shit I'm doing nagging? What about our grandchild? He's going to grow up to think shit like this is right and be in the same situation if not worse."

Joseph clicked off the television and exhaled exasperatedly as he stood up from the couch. He kissed his wife on top of her head and walked away. She called for him to come back but he didn't. He grabbed their suitcase and made his way to the guest room. He refused to put up with Tonya and her shit all night long. *She will come around eventually* he thought to himself.

"I cannot believe this asshole of a husband," Tonya said aloud. "That damn Lamar and Sonya has poisoned my baby and she will burn in hell with them." She got down on her knees and prayed for Mia. "Father, I come to you and ask that you keep your arms wrapped around my baby. Those devils are trying to grasp her into their web of lies and lust that they believe is love. I know all have sinned but it's not my daughter's fault. The temptation has gotten the best of her but I need you to bring her back to the light, Lord. In Jesus name I pray, amen.

She got up from her knees, not realizing that Lamar was watching and listening to her the entire time. He slipped back into the room unnoticed as she shut off all the lights in the living room and kitchen, before heading down the hall to her husband who had already fallen asleep waiting for her.

Chapter Six

Thanksgiving Day

These past few days have been both awkward and annoying in the polygamous household. Tonya and Joseph did decide to stick around for Thanksgiving dinner instead of going home. Joseph had lightened up to the situation of Lamar, Sonya, and his stepdaughter. Tonya on the other hand was as stubborn as a mule and had only left the room to shower and grab a food to eat. She hadn't said a word to anyone in the past couple of days, not even to Joseph and they slept together in the same room every night.

"Good morning, baby girl," Joseph said to Mia when he walked into the kitchen.

"Morning, Joseph. Would you like a cup of coffee while I make me a cup?"

"Sure, sweetheart, but I didn't know you could drink coffee while you were pregnant."

"I'm not supposed to but I need my damn coffee," she laughed. "It keeps me from feeling sluggish and I guess the baby likes it because he hasn't made me throw it up this entire time."

"That's good to know I guess. So, what are y'all plans for the day?"

"Well since Thanksgiving is in a couple of days we probably just head out and get everything we will be cooking for dinner. We have a bunch of stuff to get especially snacks for when everybody's watching football."

"You got that right, shorty, and I can't wait," Lamar said jogging into the kitchen.

"Good morning, baby," Mia said kissing him.

"Good morning, baby. Good morning, Mr. Joseph," he said looking to Joseph.

"Morning, son. Hey look I want to apologize about Tonya, and how she has been acting. We really do appreciate the hospitality, Lamar."

"It's all cool, Mr. Joseph. A lot of people don't understand our relationship from the outside looking in and are always quick to judge. We're used to it honestly," he replied.

"We definitely are," Mia replied. She put sugar and cream in three cups of coffee and handed one to each of the men then began to drink her own cup. "Babe, we gotta go and get the stuff today for Thanksgiving dinner. What time are we leaving?"

"Whenever Sonya get her butt up and get ready," L laughed.

"How is she not up yet and it was her idea to get to the grocery store as soon as they opened?" Mia asked pouring another cup of coffee and taking it into the room to Sonya. The two men just laughed.

"Women are never on time for anything," Joseph said to Lamar.

"Man you not speaking anything but the truth," Lamar said raising his mug to Joseph's and they clanked them together.

"Hey how about I join you all today? After maybe we could hit up a bar or something?"

"That's cool with me. My boys and I aren't working today because everybody is out doing what we should have done already, but Sonya and Mia always want to wait until the last minute."

"Sounds like Tonya's ass."

"I guess like mother like daughter."

"Nothing but truth my man," Joseph said and the two men let out a hearty laugh. They continued to talk while they waited for the women.

"Thanks for the coffee, Mia," Sonya said as she sat up in the bed with Mia next to her.

"No problem, babe, but we are going to have a problem if you don't get your sexy self up and we get to this store," Mia laughed.

"It's not even that damn late."

"It's almost nine o'clock, Sonya."

"Oh shit let me hurry up," Sonya said jumping up as fast as she could with her humongous belly. She took a quick shower and dressed within thirty minutes and was ready to go. She grabbed her coffee and headed to the kitchen to join Lamar, Mia, and Joseph.

"She has finally risen," Lamar joked. She walked over and kissed him after playfully punching him in the arm.

"You all crack me up, Lamar. I love it," Joseph responded as he finished up his second cup of coffee. "So what time are we heading out of this joint?"

"I'll be ready in a second, Mr. Joseph. I just need to run and take my prenatal vitamins then we can go," Sonya replied grabbing a bagel off the counter.

67   Trinity

"Oh shoot I need to take mine, too," Mia said grabbing a bagel for herself.

"That's cool. And I wish you all would stop calling me 'Mr. Joseph.' Joseph works perfectly fine," he laughed.

"Cool I can do that," Sonya said before she and Mia left the kitchen to go take their vitamin.

"We gonna be out in the car, ladies," Lamar yelled out to them. He grabbed his keys and he and Joseph made their way outside to his truck. Moments later, the two women emerged from the house and started to walk past the truck. "Where are y'all going?"

"We not riding with y'all, L," Mia responded hopping into her Charger.

"Exactly, baby, we don't wanna ride with y'all," Sonya added.

"Well just follow us then, Mia. I love y'all."

"We love you too, Daddy," they both responded in unison. They backed the car out of the driveway and Lamar did the same and followed them.

"This must be the life," Joseph said starting to start up a conversation.

"It is though. I got two smart and beautiful ladies that I love very much," Lamar responded with a smile.

"Man you got two women that can make you happy and I have one that just stresses me out," Joseph responded shaking his head.

"What you mean, Joseph? Ms. Tonya seems like she's a great woman. I mean y'all have been together for a brick."

"Yeah we have been together for many years but that woman and the way she talks down to others is depressing. And then the situation with you three, she practically chewed me out the other night because I told her I don't see a problem with it."

"I thank you for that, Joseph but if she stresses you out and makes your life a living hell, why not get a divorce?"

"It's not that simple, Youngblood. I love that woman with all my soul and my love for her hasn't driven me away yet."

"I can feel you on that because it's a headache having one woman nagging you. Imagine having to deal with two at the same time."

"Damn, Lamar. I'm gonna have to buy you a drink tonight."

"And I will gradually accept that," he laughed. They continued their conversation while still following the women as best as they could as they drove down the highway.

//

After shopping forever for the Thanksgiving items, Mia and Sonya decided to go to the nail salon for a little relaxation. Lamar and Joseph took the groceries home and put everything up. By the time they had finished everything, it was after one o'clock in the afternoon. They were enjoying a cold beer and watching the highlights from the previous night's basketball game. It was as peaceful as it could possibly be; that is until Tonya came out and decided to ruin their little fun.

"So you didn't think to wake me up or anything this morning, Joseph?" she asked standing in front of the television with her arms folded across her chest.

"I thought you needed to rest and shit, Tonya, damn," Joseph responded trying to maneuver his head around her but each way he moved, she moved as well.

"Excuse me, Ms. Tonya, we're trying to watch the highlights," Lamar said calmly.

"I don't give a shit what you're trying to do, Lamont," she yelled at him.

"My name is Lamar, Ms. Tonya," he said rising to his feet. Joseph stopped him midway and he sat back down while Joseph stood to his feet.

"Look goddamnit, nobody has time for your shit, Tonya. You have been moody and angry the past couple of days and not speaking to anybody. The least you can do is speak to the people who's home it is. Hell, you haven't even spoken to your own damn child!"

"How dare you talk to me like that, Joseph," Tonya said staring back at him with an astonished look on her face.

He looked at her like she was crazy then looked at Lamar who couldn't do anything but hunch his shoulders. He sat back down and took a couple more swigs from his beer bottle; and she continued to stand there.

"So you're not going to apologize or anything, Joseph?"

"Nope."

"You are so damn inconsiderate," she yelled again before stomping off like a child that didn't get their way. She slammed the door at the end of the hall and screamed at the top of her lungs, then silence filled the air.

"And you put up with that everyday, Joseph, man?" Lamar asked laughing.

"Every goddamn day, my man," he said taking the last swig of his brew. Lamar took the empty bottles and disposed them, bringing back four more beers, two for each of them.

"I think nightfall needs to hurry up so we can go grab a drink."

"Exactly because these beers aint cutting it for me." They continued to watch the highlights for another hour then turned on an episode of Arrow.

"You might like this show. I be having the girls watch it and they love it."

"I've seen this show a few times and I enjoy it."

"Cool," Lamar said looking at his watch. It was going on four o'clock and Sonya and Mia still wasn't back yet. He decided to give them a call and check on them.

"Hey, baby, what's up?" Mia said sweetly.

"Where y'all at? I haven't heard from y'all in a couple of hours now. Y'all better not be with no niggas," he said in a slight joking manner, but he was dead serious.

"Boy please, don't nobody want our fat pregnant asses, boo. We're just finishing up at the nail salon and on our way home."

"Goddamn that took forever."

"Well we gotta look good for you, baby. We got our nails and feet done. Plus we didn't wanna get up from that damn massage chair," Sonya said.

"You right, you right. Well hurry up and get here, ladies."

"Why is something wrong?" Sonya asked.

"Not really but Mia's mother was in here tripping a little while ago."

"Oh my goodness, I'm sorry baby."

"It's cool, baby, but me and Joseph gonna go out for drinks."

"Okay. What we gonna do about dinner?"

"Maybe you and Sonya can take your mother out for dinner or something. I don't know."

"Ughh I guess we can do that. What you think, Sonya?"

"I don't care, girl. Me and my babies just wanna eat some good food."

"I know that's right. Well we will be there shortly, boo," Mia said through the car phone.

"Okay cool. Love y'all."

"We love you, too," they both said simultaneously. They ended the call and headed to the house.

Upon arriving at the house, they could see Lamar and Joseph sitting in the living room through the picture window. Mia beeped the horn to get their attention and they both scrambled to their feet. The ladies walked into the house to be greeted by their man and Mia's stepfather.

"Damn, y'all couldn't wait for us to get back I see," Sonya said giggling and kissing Lamar after Mia.

"Y'all have no idea what we have been putting up with Mia's mom."

"That woman is gonna be the death of me one day," Joseph said shaking his head then walking out the house.

"Well hopefully she's doing a little better now," Mia said looking at everyone who remained silent. She walked further into the house and walked down the hall to the guest room.

"You two have fun," Sonya said. They said their goodbyes and left the house, ready to be away from the women and all of their hormones for a while.

Knock. Knock. Mia waited for her mother to respond before walking into the room. She could hear the television running but her mother didn't answer. She knocked again and still nothing; so she decided to enter anyway.

"Damn can't a woman have a little privacy?" Tonya said flicking the tv channels with the remote control.

"There's no privacy in my house," Mia giggled trying to break the tension in the room. Tonya looked at her with a frown and unmoving look on her face. "I see you're not in the joking mood."

"No I'm definitely not in a joking mood whatsoever, Mia," Tony replied clicking off the television and facing her daughter.

"Well, are you at least hungry, Mom?"

"Oh, now you're worried about wether I'm hungry or not, Mia? After leaving me behind, you wanna act all concerned at stuff now? Get out of my way, girl," she said brushing past Mia only to be grabbed by her arm.

"Can you stop acting like this, please? I would like for you to come out to dinner with me and Sonya."

"Oh you and your lover? I think I'll pass," she replied. They stood there in silence then Tonya's stomach growled loudly. The two women burst into laughter.

"Ma, can you stop being stubborn and just go out with us? I really want you to get along with both my girlfriend and my boyfriend because they're going to be around for a long time."

"If you say so, Mia." Tonya grabbed her purse and headed out the room with Mia on her heels. She walked past Sonya in the living and headed out the front door without even acknowledging Sonya's presence.

"I take it that she agreed to grab some food," Sonya asked handing Mia a Gatorade.

"Yep. This is going to be a long night."

"I can see it already," Sonya agreed. They headed out the door and joined Tonya at the car. Instead of riding in the front like normal, Sonya walked right to the back door of the driver's side of the car and hopped in. she didn't want anymore conflict with this woman tonight.

The three women arrived at Joe's Crab Shack in Greenbelt almost an hour later because of the evening traffic. The place was fairly crowded with other patrons but that didn't deter them from being seated moments after stepping through the door. They were seated in a booth closest to the bathroom because of Sonya and Mia having to pee every ten to fifteen minutes.

"This food is expensive," Tonya replied looking over the prices next to each item.

"Not really. We come here all the time," Sonya said opening her menu.

"I don't recall asking you anything," Tonya snapped back, silencing Sonya.

"Ma!" Mia exclaimed.

"Ma, what, Mia?"

"Excuse me for a second. I have to use the bathroom," Sonya said scooting out the booth and walking swiftly to the ladies room.

"Why the hell did you do that to her?"

"Don't you use that kind of tone with me, Mia. I am still your mother."

"Well you're surely not acting like it."

"I beg your pardon? What did I do wrong?"

"You didn't have to respond to her like that. She was just trying to have a conversation with you, Mother."

"What for? I don't want to be talking to her. She is Satan's child, sent here to do all of this fornicating between you and your man. It's bad enough you two are doing sinful acts under God's eye. And then having the nerve to bring not one, but two babies, into this world with both having two mothers. You're smarter than this, Mia."

"I'm going to pretend like you didn't just say that. If you have one more outburst like that or disrespect her, I will leave you here alone and you will not be welcomed back into our home."

"Okay okay, I will try to behave."

"Good. Thank you." Tonya motioned for the waitress to come back to the table.

"May I help you with something, Ma'am?"

"Bring me the strongest drink that you have, and keep them coming."

Later that night, around midnight, the three women were walking into the house. Mia's mother had thrown up twice after they left the restaurant and was being extremely loud. Surprisingly, after she had gotten a couple of drinks in her system, she eased up on Sonya and actually carried on conversations with her. She even managed to apologize to both Mia and Sonya for how she had been acting; explaining to them why she had acted like that in the first place. They helped her into the room and helped out of her clothes and into the bed. Lamar and Joseph still hadn't arrived home yet but Sonya and Mia didn't give a damn. They took a shower together, helping each other wash the places they couldn't reach themselves. They

75   Trinity

got in the bed wearing nothing but Lamar's oversized t-shirts. By the time the clock struck one, they were both fast asleep, laying facing one another.

/ /

Thanksgiving morning was already hectic as ever in the trio's household. It was eight o'clock in the morning and Mia's mother had them in there cooking already. Mia was cleaning the collard greens and chitterlings, while Sonya was making the potato salad and the pasta salad. Tonya was busy getting the pans of macaroni and cheese ready along with the green bean casserole. As for the men, they were doing what they did best, sleeping and staying out of the way.

"Can we please take a break, Ms. Tonya? I'm really hungry and I know Mia is as well because we haven't eaten anything yet," Sonya whined.

Tonya looked back and forth between the two women and decided to let them take a break. She told them to go rest and put their feet up for a little while. She propped pillows up for them on the sofa and handed them the remote control before heading back to the kitchen to make them a quick breakfast. After resting for about half an hour, Tonya emerged from the kitchen carrying a tray for the ladies. There was a bowl of grits for each one of them, some turkey bacon, some fruit, and orange juice along with their prenatal vitamins. They tore into the food like cannibals as soon as she sat it down on the sofa. The smell of the breakfast had awaken the men and they were both headed into the kitchen simultaneously.

"I smell food. Where's my plate?" Joseph said with a hearty laugh as Lamar trailed behind him.

"I know you two better hurry up and get out of the kitchen so we can get back to work in a bit," Tonya scolded her husband. Lamar laughed as he stuffed a spoonful of grits in his mouth.

"Thank you, Ms. Tonya," Lamar said. He stood up to go see his ladies. He kissed them both on the forehead and snatched a couple pieces of fruit before heading back to his food.

Trinity

"No problem, Lamar, but we are gonna have a problem if you take food from my grandbabies again," she said sitting a bowl of fruit next to both he and Joseph's bowl of grits. Joseph and Lamar exchanged looks, then looked behind them and exchanged looks with Sonya and Mia. "Did I say something wrong?"

"You said grandbabies, Tonya," Joseph informed her.

"I know exactly what I said. Those children can have two grandmothers and two grandfathers, even in a situation like this. And let's not forget Lamar's parents as well," she said smiling. Joseph stood to kiss his wife and Mia and Sonya were wobbling into the kitchen to do the same.

"You're alright with me, Ms. Tonya."

"Thank you, Lamar. Now it's almost noon," she said looking at her watch. "You two need to get down to the liquor store and get beer and drinks for later because nobody is going anywhere when the game comes on."

"You got that right," Joseph agreed. "After we finish, we will go ahead and head out. Just write down what all you want us to get."

"Already done," Tonya replied handing them a list of liquor and other alcoholic beverages that they needed to pick up. They hurried up and finished and went to get ready, an hour later, they were heading out the door to the liquor store.

"Time to get back to work ladies. Your break time is up," Tonya replied clapping her hands in the air. The women stood and drug their feet across the hardwood floor back into the kitchen. For the next few hours they continued to cook and clean as they went. Finally, around four o'clock, they were able to shower again and get dressed before the guests arrived in the next couple of hours.

"Your mom is actually not that bad, Mia," Sonya replied putting on her purple PINK sweat suit.

"Naw she's not. I think seeing you and finding out that I have both a girlfriend and a boyfriend kind of shook her a little."

"A little? Baby, you almost sent your Mama to an early grave," Sonya laughed.

"Yeah that sounds about right," Mia agreed laughing as she put on her pink PINK sweat suit. They both put on their Ugg boots because they didn't want to put on sneakers; nobody had time to be dealing with their feet hurting.

"Damn y'all looking like fine wine," Lamar said walking into the room and closing the door behind him and locking it. He walked over to them and kissed them both, damn near causing them to choke on his tongue as he stuck it down their throats.

"Don't be getting us all hot and bothered, Daddy," Sonya said between heavy breaths.

"Why not? Y'all my girlfriends," he replied pulling on their waistbands at the same time.

"What are you doing?" Mia asked allowing him to pull her closer to him.

"I just want a quickie ," he said licking his lips at them.

"People are showing up and more people are coming. We can't do this right now," Sonya whispered.

"We can do whatever we want. This is our damn house," he replied. He had both ladies place their hands on the bed and he pulled their pants down to their ankles. He leaned Mia over first, getting the angle right before pushing the head deep into her wet pussy. She moaned out and quickly threw a hand over her mouth to block out the noise. It was turning Sonya on and she couldn't wait to be touched any longer. She slipped out of her boots and kicked her sweatpants from around her ankles. She laid down on the bed in front of Mia, putting one of her breasts into her mouth, sucking on her nipple. Mia leaned over a little more and began to lick and finger Sonya's pussy, letting her sweet juices pour onto her lips. Sonya moaned softly and then pulled Mia in to a kiss. After Mia had come all over Lamar, it was now Sonya's turn. They quickly switched positions, not trying to miss a beat. Lamar banged Sonya's back out, and she feasted on Mia's pussy. Within minutes, both Sonya and Mia were squirting all over the place. Both women positioned themselves on their knees comfortably in front of Lamar, catching his hot semen as he shot it down their throats. They took turns sucking the excess cum from his manhood before he helped them to their feet. He adjusted his clothes and they went to do a quick wash and brush their teeth again. They put their clothes back on, sprayed a little perfume, then headed out the room to welcome the guests as they arrived.

/ /

The huge dining room table was surrounded by many relatives, friends, and a few neighbors, as they gathered to join hands and to say grace and to say what they were all thankful for.

"Everyone join hands and bow your heads please," Tonya said aloud over the mild chatter in the room which subsided within seconds. Everyone in the room had a hand in theirs and closed their eyes and bowed their heads as she began. "Heavenly Father, we come to you today with many thanks on this glorious Thanksgiving day. We pray that you continue to bless everyone in attendance here with us today. Continue to bless their families and bless them with nothing but success. For those that are less fortunate, I pray that you will bless them with a hot meal today and a comfy bed to sleep on tonight. In Jesus name, we pray, Amen." They all said 'Amen' in unison and then began to go around the circle to say what they were thankful for. And again, Tonya began. "I am thankful to be alive and healthy today. I am also thankful that my daughter will be blessing me with my first grandchild next month and Sonya will be blessing me with two grandchildren."

Now it was Mia's turn to state what she was thankful for. "I'm thankful to be blessed with my little boy and also for my boyfriend, Lamar, and my girlfriend, Sonya. I am just happy to be surrounded by loved ones today," she smiled.

"Okay, I guess it's my turn," Lamar replied. "I'm happy and thankful to have been blessed with these two beautiful women that make my life complete. And even more so, we will be having three additions to our family in just a few weeks; two boys and one girl. I'm so excited, probably more excited than them. But, um, yeah, that's what I'm thankful for."

"Well, I must say I'm thankful for the same things my partners are thankful for," Sonya laughed. "I, um, have never been so thankful in my life until I met these two. Ever since, my life has been so much better and filled with a lot of love." They continued to go around the room until each and every person said what they were thankful for. Once they were finished, it was time to eat. Mia and Sonya made Lamar's plate as he and the rest of the guys gathered in the living room to watch the football game. After they served their man his food, they went back to make theirs and joined the other women in the dining room. Everything was going all nice and smooth until Sonya's mother, Amelia, decided to speak her mind.

"How can you people condone such nonsense?" she said in her strong Spanish accent. "I love my daughter but I will not tolerate her bringing my two grandchildren into such a mess."

"Mama, please calm down. You have been drinking too much and you are starting to act up," Sonya replied reaching out to snatch the tequila from her mother's hand, but she snatched it back.

"No, no, Sonya, you will not blame the tequila on this. You are coming with me right now and we are leaving." She grabbed Sonya by the arm and Mia pulled her other arm, pulling her back to her. A split second had passed and Sonya's mother was in Mia's face now. "This is you and that negro boyfriend of yours fault." At the sound of the word 'negro,' silence filled the room and all eyes were set dead on all of the commotion. "I should slap you, you little punta," Amelia replied raising her hand. Before she could land her hand on Mia's face, Tonya was up in her face with the knife they used to carve the turkey at her throat.

"If you put your motherfucking hands on my child, you will regret it and I will slice your damn neck open. If you wanna act bad, try me. That's all I want you to do is try me, woman." You could see the fear in Amelia's eyes as Tonya glared at her. Both Sonya and Mia tried to pry the knife from Tonya's hand but it didn't work. One of Mia's aunts quickly ran to get Lamar and Joseph, and the other guys followed behind to see the action. "Tonya what are you doing?" Joseph asked frightened.

"This crazy woman was about to put her hands on my baby. "Baby, Mia is a grown woman and can protect herself. I know that but while I'm here I'm doing the protecting. Now if this heifer got a problem with this situation then she can leave, but Sonya and those babies are staying here."

"Tonya? You were just acting like this just the other day. Now what makes it any difference?" Joseph asked.

"Two things made a difference. Number one, this is what makes my child happy and I have to learn to deal with it because I love her. Number two, this chick tried to lay hands on my daughter and that's not gonna happen on my watch."

"Ms. Tonya, hand me the knife," Lamar said grabbing her hand. Tonya would not let up but when Mia asked her to let it go, she slowly eased her fingers from around the handle and let it drop into Lamar's hand. As soon as it was out of her grasp, Amelia grabbed the tequila bottle and smashed it over Tonya's head. Not succeeding in taking her down with that, Tonya quickly tackled Amelia into the dining room table, causing it to break under them from the weight they put on top. Tonya and Amelia both were exchanging blows to one another's face and food was flying everywhere. They were hitting each other with legs from the turkey, Tonya broke

Amelia's gravy boat over her head, and Amelia slammed the entire pan of macaroni and cheese onto the top of Tonya's head. After a while, Lamar and Joseph separated the women and told Amelia that she had to leave. She gathered up her belongings and tried to give her daughter a kiss goodbye but Sonya didn't budge. Amelia looked at everyone in the room and tears dropped as Sonya turned her back and walked away. Her mother walked the opposite way and headed towards the front door. She took one more look back and left the house. She hopped in her Prius and left to go back home, feeling mad, stupid and embarrassed. But no matter what, she knew deep down she was going to always love her daughter regardless.

Chapter Seven
The Big Fight

L ater that night Sonya had stayed up alone so she could watch a little tv and clear her head of the night's catastrophe. She wanted so bad for one of her lovers to come and check on her but they were so busy in the room having sex. While she was shedding emotional tears in the living room by herself, Mia and Lamar were in the bedroom; making the bed squeak and filling the room with moans and the sweet smell of sex in the atmosphere. Her mother had been blowing her phone up for the past four hours and it wasn't doing anything but pissing her off even more. She had answered the first few times but all they did was argue and go back and forth with one another and then hanging up on each other. By the fifth time Amelia had called, Sonya had blocked her number. Now, determined to talk to her daughter, Amelia continued to call Sonya's cell phone. Her phone was ringing again and for the umpteenth time, she ignored it and checked the time on her phone screen; it read 3:15 a.m. She decided to just put her phone on do not disturb mode and avoid her calls altogether until she felt like talking to her mom. She wiped her face and paused the movie Selena so she wouldn't miss any parts of her favorite movie. She retreated to the kitchen to grab something to drink and snack on. After scanning the fridge for a few moments, she decided on a bottle of apple juice, some fruit and some leftover sweet potato pie. As soon as she closed the fridge and turned around, she had bumped into Mia and ended up dropping everything.

"Shit," she said before dropping to her knees to pick up her items.

"I am so sorry, Sonya. I didn't mean to scare you," Mia replied as she helped Sonya back to her feet then ran to grab the broom and dustpan to clean up the pieces of pie crust that fell out the metal tray.

"You didn't technically scare me but you did startle me a little. What are you doing up anyway, Mia? From the way you were in there screaming, I would have thought you was in there knocked out calling the hogs," Sonya replied sarcastically with a smirk on her face. She was sitting down eating her fruit and pie now.

Mia just laughed gingerly and sat on a stool next to Sonya. "Yeah I would have been but I wanted to check on you and make sure you were doing okay after everything that had happened earlier," she replied grabbing a slice of pie from the tray for herself.

"Well that is very noble of you to check on me after all these hours." Mia saw when Sonya had rolled her eyes up in her head and was going to ignore it at first, but her ghetto and ratchet side surfaced quicker than she had hoped for. She hopped off the stool carefully with her big belly and stared right at Sonya.

"Do you have a problem with me, Sonya? Like, on the real, is there something you got on your chest that you wanna tell me? If so, I'm all ears, Boo Boo."

Sonya looked at her through the slits in her eyes and Mia stared back with eyes of anger. Sonya sat there on the stool and taunted Mia for a while with her snacking and drinking in utter silence. Once she finished everything, she got off her stool and wobbled over to the trash can and threw out her garbage. She walked over and stood in front of Mia and smiled. "Mia, yes, I do have a problem with you. You always walking around like little Miss Perfect and acting like Lamar only belongs to you. He belongs to us both or did you forget?"

Mia chuckled a little. "Us? Us, really? First of all, if your brain can go back that far, you will remember that Lamar found you and brought you here to be in our relationship. It wasn't the other way around, baby. I'm gonna be here forever if you need to be reminded. Besides I'm carrying his child."
"So am I dumbass," Sonya said placing her hand on her stomach. "Well, I'm carrying two of his kids which makes me more important," Sonya added laughing and smiling. You could see Mia's blood boiling and she was trying to keep it together.

"Bitch I will kill your Spanish ass and won't even second guess myself. Try me if you want too," Mia said through clenched teeth.

"I don't have time for this little girl bullshit," Sonya said bumping Mia with her shoulder as she made her way past her and out the kitchen. She spun around and looked back at Mia with a smile plastered on her face. "Oh and by the way, Lamar had already known me. We have been fucking around for a little over two years before he introduced us. The only reason he brought me home is because I threatened to come here and tell you about us. Well now I'm here, and it's just a matter of time before it will only be me and him." She turned back around to retreat from the kitchen once again.

"You skanky bitch," Mia replied before charging towards Sonya and grabbing her by the back of the head, wrapping her hair around her fist. Sonya tried to free herself from Mia's grasp but it worked to no avail. Mia continued to hold Sonya by the hair as she grabbed the front of her shirt, swinging her around so her face could come in contact with the granite countertop. She unraveled Sonya's hair from her fist and observed all the blood trickling from Sonya's nose and lips.

"Mia have you lost your fucking mind?" Sonya screamed.
"I haven't lost it yet bitch, but I'm definitely on the verge," she replied. She tried to get at Sonya again only to be grabbed up by Lamar and tossed across the kitchen floor.

" have lost y'all rabbit ass minds? What the fuck is going on?"
"She started. No she started," both Sonya and Mia replied pointing fingers at one another.

"What the fuck are y'all in third grade? Y'all supposed to be fucking adults," he barked and the room became still. "Sonya tell me what happened."
Sonya grabbed a napkin and ran it under the faucet water. She wiped the blood residue from her face before telling her side of the story. "Well, I was out here chilling and minding my business. Then Mia came out here

accusing me of ruining y'all relationship and telling me I had to leave. And when I told her I was gonna tell you what she said, she attacked me from behind," Sonya replied through fake sobs.

"Oh that is bullshit, Sonya, and you fucking know it. She told me all about y'all before you had brought her home and she was rubbing in the fact that she was carrying two children for you and I was only carrying one," Mia said through teary eyes.

Lamar looked back and forth between them as they both became silent. "I know it had better be a better reason than that shit, Mia. I know good and well that you ain't almost risk the lives of my children over some dumb shit like that. I just know that's not the case."

"Your children? Nigga did you forget I was carrying your child, too?" she yelled at him.

"No I didn't forget but it still doesn't make it right. You need to apologize to Sonya right now."

"I'm not apologizing to that bitch. You love that bitch more than me, Lamar, huh? Motherfucker I been there for you all these years and you gonna choose this hoe over me."

"I'm choosing the lives of my kids and if you gonna be doing this type of shit, you need to leave now."

"Leave? You putting me out for this bitch, too? Nigga you got me fucked up," she screamed and ran towards Lamar and throwing blows at his head that he was blocking. He managed to grab both of her arms and pull her towards the front door.

"Open the door, Sonya," he yelled at Sonya. She obliged with no problem whatsoever. Lamar pushed Mia outside, causing her to fall to her stomach. He quickly locked the front door in case she decided to try and come back in. He could hear Mia yelling and screaming and crying loudly outside. He made it to the bedroom and began throwing all of her belongings out the window. Nosey neighbors began to gather around outside and peep through the blinds. A couple of people tried to help Mia but she just kept putting up her charade. Lamar had had enough of the bullshit. He called the police and told them that Mia had tried to assault him and they came out as soon as they could. Once they arrived, they spoke to both Lamar and Sonya and asked for the statements. In the end, Mia was carried off to jail and Sonya and Lamar watched as the police car disappeared in the distance.

/ /

Several weeks had passed by and neither Lamar nor Sonya had seen or heard anything from Mia. For an entire week after Lamar kicked her out the house, she had called all day and all night; damn near every single minute. She had gotten blocked and then she just started calling from random numbers. The shit had gotten so ridiculous that Lamar changed the numbers to both of their cell phones, as well as the house number. Today was the first day that Lamar would be leaving Sonya home alone but he didn't wanna leave. She would be delivering any day soon and he didn't want to miss the birth of his twins. He thought it over and hoped that Mia would call and let him know when she went into labor so he could be there as well.

"Ahhhh. Oh shit," Sonya yelled out in pain. Lamar ran from the bedroom to the living room when he heard her screams.

"Baby are you okay?" he asked rushing to her side and holding her up as she held onto the counter.

"I'm having really bad labor pains again."

"Do you wanna go back to the hospital?"

"No, Babe, remember what the doctor said last week? It's probably just those damn Braxton hicks contractions again," she replied struggling to make it over to the couch with the assistance of Lamar.

Trinity

"Are you sure you're gonna be okay?"

"Yes, L, just go. I will call you if I need you back home."

"You better. I'm only gonna be an hour away so just let me know."

"I will. We love you, baby," Sonya said softly rubbing her belly.

"I love all three of y'all, too," he replied. He leaned over to kiss her lips and kiss her stomach. He grabbed his stuff and left to get on the road.
Sonya was a little sad to be left alone in the house. She usually had Mia to be by her side and keep her company, but that's in the past. She had to come to the realization that Mia was gone and not coming back. As she flicked through the channels and thought about the entire ordeal, a smile crept upon her face.

"Lamar is all mine and I don't have to worry about sharing him anymore," she said aloud.

Eventually she found a movie that had piqued her interest. She had no idea on earth what she was watching but she was really enjoying it. As the end credits rolled up the screen, she wiped the tears that ran down her face from the movie's ending. The house phone rang and it startled her for a second. She wobbled over to retrieve it and as soon as she answered, the person on the other end hung up the phone in her ear.

"They must've had the wrong number," she thought. She decided to keep the phone with her so she wouldn't have to keep walking to get it. She decided since she was up she would get a snack. She scanned the fridge and found a bag of grapes. She rinsed the entire bag and placed them in a bowl. As she was walking back to the living room, the phone rang again, causing her to jump and almost dropping her bowl.

"Hello?" she quickly answered the phone, but nobody responded. "Hellooo?" she repeated because she had heard heavy breathing on the other end. "Look stop fucking calling my house you bastard," she replied before disconnecting the call.

When she got back in the living room, she grabbed her phone to call Lamar. "Hey, Baby, what's up?" he replied as soon as he answered the phone.

"Nothing, Babe, I was just checking on you to make sure you were okay."

"Yeah I'm good, love. What's wrong with you though? You sound all out of breath and shit. Is everything okay? Is it the babies?" he rambled.

"No nothing like that. It's just I been getting some weird phone calls and-"

Sonya's conversation with Lamar had gotten briefly interrupted by the sound of the alarm on Sonya's car.

"What's that noise, babe?" Lamar asked.

"It's just the car, L, no biggie," she replied as she went towards the front door to grab her car keys. She peeped out the window to make sure the coast was clear before opening the door. Once she saw there was nothing outside to fear, she quickly opened the door to try and turn the alarm off. After a few tries, it turned off and she shut the door and locked it.

"Is everything okay, Sonya?"

"Yes, Lamar, everything is just fine. I just think I need a new battery for my car key."

"Well we will handle that when I get back. Did you make sure to set the alarm?" he asked.

"I'm doing it right now as we speak."

"Cool cool. So, what are you gonna do for the rest of the night?"

"Well, I'm about to hop in the shower and then go to bed. I just wish you were here to hold us, baby," she replied sadly into the phone.

"Well, baby, I will be back in two days but if need be, I can come home tomorrow."

"Stop it, Lamar. The babies and I will be perfectly fine while you're gone, okay?"

"Okay, boo."

"I love you, L."

"I love you, too, Sonya."

/ /

As it grew later into the wee hours of the morning, Mia just couldn't sleep. She had been tossing and turning all night as pains shot through her abdomen.

"Aahhhh," she screamed out in pain for the umpteenth time that night. Her mom ran into the room and turned on the bright ceiling light.

"What's the matter, Mia? Is it the baby? Are you ready to deliver?" she rambled on a mile a minute.

"I don't know. I'm just in a lot of pain and it hurts so bad." Mia tried to stand up but doubled over from the excruciating pain and dropped to the floor.

Her mother grabbed the phone and called 911 and asked that they send the paramedics as soon as they possibly could. They informed her that they were being dispatched and would arrive roughly in about 15-20 minutes. Mia fought through the contractions as she grabbed a pair of sweatpants and a tank top to put on. As she did this, her mother ran into her room to get dressed. Moments had passed and they were ready but there was still no sign of the paramedics.

"Where the fuck are they?" Mia's mom yelled at the too of her lungs.

"Ma, please calm down because you are not making this any easier." She pulled out her phone and started dialing.

"Are you calling them, Mia?"

"No. I'm calling Lamar."

"What are you calling that piece of shit for? He doesn't give a damn about you or that baby, Mia."

"It's still his child, mother," she replied rolling her eyes up in her head. "That boy is gonna be your downfall. You mark my words," she said as she retreated from the room.

You have reached the voicemail box for L. Please leave your message after the tone. Mia had dialed Lamar's number several more times only to get the same message. She blocked her number and called and he immediately sent it to voicemail.

"You fucking bastard," she screamed. She grabbed her mother's cell phone and texted Lamar and informed him that the baby was coming and to meet her at the hospital. As soon as she hung up the phone, she heard the ambulance outside. Moments later, heavy footsteps ascended the stairs.

They entered the room and put her on a stretcher and quickly rushed her down the stairs and out to the ambulance. She looked around for her mother as they were getting ready to shut the doors.

"Hold on, i'm coming, too," Mia's mother exclaimed. She and Mia looked at each other and smiled. All the stuff they have been through it still amazed

Trinity

Mia how her mother was still there for her. Her mother pushed the paramedic over demanding she sat closer to her daughter so she could hold her hand.

"I'm so scared, Mom," Mia said through tears. "It hurts so bad."
"I know baby, I know, but it will be okay. Just think about the most precious reward you will get after all of this madness is over." Mia grasped her moms hand tighter each time a contraction hit. They were getting closer and closer.

Mia's mother yelled at the ambulance driver to hurry up before or he was gonna need a stretcher next.

✳✳✳✳

Across the way, Sonya was struggling all alone with the twins in the house. She had called Lamar several times and left several messages as well but nothing. The only difference between Mia and Sonya right now was the fact that Sonya was all alone. She didn't have Mia to help her, no Lamar, nor her own mother.
After about ten minutes of enduring the excruciating pain and trying to get out the bed, Sonya had finally made it to her feet.

Her face was covered in tears from the pain. As she clicked on the bedside lamp, she grabbed her phone and called for an ambulance and they told her it would be about fifteen or twenty minutes. She looked at the bed and noticed all the water in the bed. *Lamar is going to kill me* she laughed to herself trying to smile through the contractions.

She tried to make her way around the room to gather up her and the twins's hospital items. She wished Lamar was there because she ended up having to use a bigger bag than she thought. As she tried her best to hurry and pack the bag, she was startled by her phone ringing. She looked at the caller id and saw that it was Lamar.

"Oh my God, Baby, where are you? Are you on your way home? What's going on?" she rambled on a mile a minute as she continued to cry hysterically.

"Baby, baby, baby, calm down. Take a deep breath. Everything will be okay. Sonya," Lamar said calmly into the phone. Sonya immediately got quiet and calmed down a little as she was told.

"Okay, L, I'm calm," she replied trying her best to breathe through the contractions.

"That's good, Baby. Don't worry I am on my way there. I will just meet you at the hospital because I would be closer than me coming home."
"Baby, I'm so scared. I just wish you were here with me right now. I really need you, Lamar," she cried and sniffled.

"I know, Baby, I know. I am here and I always will be."

"I know you will be, Daddy," she replied. She heard hard rapping at the door and made her way as quickly as she could and opened the door for paramedics.

"Hello, Ma'am. Were you the one that called for an ambulance?" the young white boy asked.

"What the fuck do you think?" Sonya screamed at him pointing to her overgrown belly. The other paramedics giggled as the white kid turned red in the cheeks.

"Enough with the shenanigans, we need to get this woman to the hospital," a female EMT said as she bumrushed through the guys. She and another EMT worked together to place Sonya on the stretcher. They made their way to the ambulance and rushed her inside.

As they rode to the hospital, the female paramedic asked Sonya the usual questions as far as her birthday, how far the contractions were apart, and other shit Sonya did not care to answer at the moment.

The only thing she was worried about at the moment was getting to the hospital and delivering her two bundles of joy. She smiled within as she thought about how great it would be to finally hold her prince and princess in her arms. Just the thought of that was causing her to forget about the agonizing contractions she was currently having; she couldn't wait. She just hoped that Lamar made it in time because as much pain as she was in, she was determined not to deliver those babies unless he was present. There were no ifs, ands, or buts about it.

Chapter Eight
The Hospital

Mia was way beyond the point of being pissed the fuck off. Not only did the dumbasses hit a few potholes on the way to the hospital, they still had her just lounging around on a stretcher in the maternity wing. They said she had to wait for a room to clear before she could go in. Her mother was cussing everybody out from the receptionist to the janitor about getting her daughter into a room and delivering her grandson. They had her sitting in an almost upright position just enough to see who came in and out of the maternity wing. As her mother talked to her and caressed her head, she noticed a smile had crept up on her daughter's face. She smiled at her but her smile quickly vanished when she looked into the direction of where her daughter was looking. And low and behold, Lamar was rushing from the elevator over to the receptionist desk. He hadn't even noticed Mia lying on the stretcher off to the side of the hallway.

"Hello, Sir, how may I help you?" the older lady asked Lamar.

"Yeah, I'm looking for my girlfriend."

"Okay, no problem, Sir. What is her name?"

"Her name is-"

"Baby, I'm right here," Mia called out. She waved her hands as best as she could so he could notice her when he turned in her direction. He saw that was Mia instead of Sonya. He thanked the receptionist lady and steadfastly walked over to Mia and her mom.

"Mia what are you doing here?" he asked.

"What do you mean? It's obviously I'm about to deliver our son."

"What the fuck do you think she's doing here you piece of shit?" Mia's mother yelled at him. "This is all your fault. You did this to my baby and ruined her future with your stupid ways," she replied as she poked him in the chest pushing him away.

"Mom, what are you doing? He came to be here by my side for the baby. Besides I love him, Mom."

"Oh hush your mouth, child. You don't know what love is dealing with a man while he dealing with another woman."

"Just tell her, Lamar. Tell her you love me and that you're here for us," she begged.

"Mia I'm sorry but I didn't come here for you."

"What? What do you mean?"

Just as a doctor came to take Mia to a room, she noticed them bringing Sonya in. She cried as her heart broke into a million pieces as she watched the love of her life, rush to be at the side of another woman. *I was here first* Mia thought to herself. Tears streamed down her face as she was being pushed away.
"Wait!" Lamar yelled at the doctor pushing Mia's stretcher down the hall. "I want both of my girlfriends in the same room delivering my children."
Everyone in earshot stopped in their tracks and transpired what he just said.
"I don't want that bitch in the room with me," Sonya yelled at the top of her lungs holding her stomach.
"I don't want that whore anywhere near my daughter or my grandson. Nor do I want that trash of a man near them either."
"Look I could care less what is going on in you guys' private lives but we need to get both of these women to a room because they both are ready to

deliver," Sonya's doctor said. Mia's doctor obliged and told him to follow him and Mia's mom to Room 20.

****

"Push, Baby, you can do it," was all Lamar kept repeating back and forth between both ladies. Mia's mother kept trying to cool her daughter down by feeding her ice chips as she pushed repeatedly. Lamar was running himself ragged trying to be by both of their side. Deep down he wanted to be there for both of them, just Sonya more.

"I see a head," Mia's doctor yelled. Both Lamar and Mia's mom scrambled to stand behind the doctor. "One more push should do it, Mia."
"Aaaarrrrggggghhhhh," Mia screamed as she did a huge push. Seconds passed by and she heard the loud cries of her newborn son. She cried tears of joy as she watched them weigh her baby boy.

"You did it baby girl," Mia's mother said rubbing her daughter's hair.
"You did it, Baby," Lamar said kissing Mia on the lips. It had caught both of them off guard for a second but Mia still smiled. She hoped that this meant they were back together now.

"Sir, we need you over here," the doctor yelled for Lamar to come back on the other side of the curtain.

"I'll be back," he told Mia as he rushed over to Sonya. And once again, Mia's mother couldn't do anything but roll her eyes.

"What the hell is going on, Doc? Why aren't my babies here yet, man?" Lamar yelled at him as he pushed him a little.

"Please refrain from putting your hands on me," the doctor said standing to his feet and standing a few inches above Lamar. Lamar eyeballed him but then calmed down because this was not the time nor the place for this. Any other time, Lamar would have probably busted a cap in his ass. "Anyway, there is no way we will be able to deliver both of these children.

She has been pushing since she been here and nothing. So we can only do the caesarean section on your girlfriend."

"That's fine. Do whatever you have to do or there will hell to pay."

"Nurse can you please give Sonya an epidural please?" he replied ignoring Lamar's comment.

"No problem, doctor." She put the medicine into the syringe and Lamar and the doctor safely placed Sonya on her side and prepared her for the injection.

"I'm so scared, Baby," Sonya cried looking into Lamar's eyes.

"I know, Boo, but I promise everything will be okay."

"Take a deep breath, Sonya," the nurse replied.
Sonya did as she was told but as soon as she felt the needle enter through her skin, she yelled out in pain. "Aaaahhhhh, fuck."

"It's okay, Sonya, it's all over now," Lamar reassured her.

"As soon as the drugs take effect, we will move along with the procedure."

"Cool, cool," Lamar replied. He stood there next to Sonya holding her hand and caressing her head lovingly.

"I wish my mother was here," she said.

"She doesn't need to be here, Sonya. As long as I'm here, that's all that matters." He kissed Sonya on the head and they waited patiently for the epidural 2 kick in.

Ten minutes had passed by before the epidural took full effect on Sonya's body. The doctor put the screen up so she couldn't see what was going on but Lamar was watching every bit of it. He watched as the doctor picked up the surgical steel scalpel and made an incision in Sonya's stomach. He opened it up and did another incision in her uterus, this time horizontally. He looked on as he seen one baby being pulled out and handed off to a nurse. Seconds later, his son was making his way into the world. Just as before, he smiled and kissed Sonya like he had done Mia.

The doctors and nurses congratulated both Mia and Sonya on giving birth to healthy children. Mia had given birth to a seven pound baby boy and Sonya had given birth to two 5 pound babies. This was the happiest day of both of these women's lives. The staff told them both to try and rest in a little while. They handed both Sonya and Lamar a baby after they sanitized their hands and Mia was able to hold her son as well. As soon as the door to their room closed, Mia's mom snatched back the curtain and began to rip into Lamar's ass yet again.

"Well, I hope you're happy with your goddamn self."
"As a matter of fact I'm ecstatic," he replied sarcastically as he rocked his daughter.

"You are a piece of shit, Lamar. I knew it from the first time I saw you. You ain't shit and ain't never gonna be shit," she rambled on. Lamar let her continue her rant until she pushed him as he held his daughter. He quickly grabbed her up by her throat with one hand as he held the baby in the other arm.
"Look you judgmental bitch, you wasn't saying all this shit when it was beneficial to you," he replied through clenched teeth. "Who the fuck did you call when you needed money for bills or groceries? Me! So don't you dare stand in my motherfucking presence passing judgement. Whether you like it or not, I'm gonna be around regardless." Mia's mom tried to pry his fingers from her throat but it worked to no avail. He looked over at Mia who was crying silent tears. He instantly dropped her mother from his grasp and walked over to Mia and apologized.

"I'm so sorry, Baby. You know I didn't mean it. She pushed me while I was holding the baby and-"

"It's okay, L, I understand. It's okay," she kept reassuring him. He kissed her on the lips and grabbed their son from her arms. "Can I hold her?" she asked Lamar. They both looked over at Sonya and she hesitated for a few minutes before reluctantly nodding her head.

"We're a family," Sonya replied.

Mia managed to get up and stand to her feet. She grabbed the baby from Lamar's arms and they both walked together over to Sonya. Mia passionately kissed Sonya and Sonya's energy matched. "Damn I missed you, Sonya. And I'm sorry for everything," Mia responded.

"I missed you, too, and I'm sorry as well," Sonya replied. Lamar kissed them both the same way they had just kissed each other."

"Sonya's right. We are a family and I love you both very much," Lamar said to his girlfriends.

"We love you, too," they replied in unison.

They put all three babies together and took so many pictures. They all agreed that they all looked like Lamar. In the background, Mia's mother was gathering her things and stopped in front of the little family.

"You're all fucking sick and going straight to hell," she screamed as she stormed out of the room.

"We'll be sure to save you a seat, Ms. Jacobs," Lamar yelled behind her. The trio erupted in laughter for a few minutes before going back to admire their beautiful creations that they were blessed with.

✳✳✳✳

Later that day, after both ladies had eaten their dinner, they practiced teaching their babies how to latch onto the nipple for feeding. Reluctantly they both got it down pact within a few moments.

"I hope them babies save some milk for me," Lamar laughed and joked.

Trinity

"You must gonna be sucking the milk from Mia's titties because these two are damn near sucking me dry already," Sonya replied and they all laughed.

"You surely can have some milk, Daddy," Mia said in her soft voice.
"Changing the conversation, what are we gonna name these little people?" Sonya interrupted.

"That's a good question, Sonya. I was thinking naming my son Lamar Anthony Washington, Jr.," Mia replied with a big smile spread across her face.
Sonya looked at her crazily as she cleared her throat. "And what makes your kid so special to be his Jr?"

"Obviously because my son was born first," Mia said with a sarcastic matter of factly chuckle.

"That don't mean a motherfucking thing, sweetheart. All that means was your pussy was wide enough for a baby to slip out," Sonya replied rolling her eyes.

"It's not my fault you took the easy way out and got cut the fuck open like a damn animal."

"Enough!" Lamar yelled at the top of his lungs. "We just got back good and you two dumbasses wanna act like fucking children over some damn names. Grow the fuck up! And, Mia, I wouldn't say another word because your ass can go back with your fucking mother after you're discharged," he said when he saw that she was about to say something back. The glare he had given her made her think twice before opening her mouth. "Now that we have all calmed the fuck down, we will name these kids. "Neither of the boys will be named after me," he said looking back and forth between them.

"I don't want them to be anything like me. I want them to do and be better. Do I make myself clear, ladies?" he asked sternly.

"Clear," Sonya replied.

"Crystal," Mia added.
"Okay, now, let's get back to what's important-our kids. Because honestly, you two motherfuckers aren't important right now acting like two damn 5-year-old children. All I know is that I want all of them to have my last name and that is not up for debate. Mia?" he said looking her way. "You were my girlfriend first so we're gonna name our son first."

"That's perfectly fine with me, Baby," Mia smiled. Sonya sucked her teeth and rolled her eyes. Lamar looked her way and his eyes dared her to utter a single word. Instead, she shifted her eyes and diverted them to the baby in her arms.

"Okay, let's see. What should we call you, little man?" Lamar asked rocking the baby in his arms. After pondering his thoughts for a few moments the perfect name came to mind. "I think we should name you Royal Xavier Washington. How do you like that name, Mia?"

"I love it, Baby. Now, what about this little princess?" she asked tapping the baby's nose with the tip of her finger.

"Yeah, what will we name our kids?" Sonya asked sarcastically.

"Anyway," Lamar stated shaking his head at Sonya's antics. "I think her name should be Princess Amani Washington and his name should be Prince Aaron Washington. How do those sound?"

"I love them both, just like I love you," Sonya smiled looking down at her son.

"I love you, too, Baby; without a doubt."

"I know."

"I love you, too, Mia."

"I love you more, Lamar."

****

The next day had arrived and Mia was discharged and sent home, but Sonya, on the other hand, had to stay an extra day because of her receiving a C-section. She was a little pissed because Mia got to go home and have Lamar all to herself. She hated that but she knew she didn't really have much of a choice. They all said their 'goodbyes' and Mia, Lamar, and baby Royal left the hospital.

The car ride home seemed like it was taking longer than it usually did. Lamar had the music playing at a low volume and was texted somebody back consistently. Mia was sitting in the back seat with Royal damn near breaking her neck trying to see who was texting her man so fucking much. It wasn't Sonya because she had been given some medicine to deal with her pain and it put her out soon after they left her. And for certain it wasn't her or none of his boys because for one, she was with him; and two his friends never texted back that quickly. *It must be another woman* Mia thought to herself. *Damn that privacy screen* she said to herself. She smiled to herself when she realized she knew his passcode. She was gonna get her hands on that phone before the night was over.

Lamar pulled up into the driveway and quickly hopped out and opened Mia's door. He helped her out and reached inside the car and grabbed Royal and the hospital bag. Mia was a little impressed how he was managing to hold the bag, the baby in the car seat, and holding the key to open the front door.

"I can open the door if you want me to, L."

"I got it," he shouted.

"I was just trying to help, Lamar, damn. You didn't have to yell at me like that," Mia said sadly.

103   Trinity

"I'm sorry, Baby," he said sincerely as he pushed open the door and continued to juggle the bag and the car seat. He dropped the bag on the floor by the front door and took Royal straight to the nursery; Mia followed right behind him practically walking on his heels.

"Wow, it looks amazing in here," Mia said in astonishment. Lamar and Sonya had added shelves to the walls and they housed stuffed animals and books for us to read to the babies. It had two rocking chairs and three cribs; it even had a section with giant fuzzy pillows stacked into a makeshift bed. *I guess that's for if we get tired and don't wanna leave the children* Mia thought.
"I want you to get some rest while Royal is sleeping, Mia. I have some errands to run and I will be back shortly."

"But I'm not even tired, Bae," she replied in a whining tone.
"What did I say?" he responded towering over her small frame. She knew not to test him.
"Okay, Lamar, I will get some rest. Do you know what time you will probably be back? I wanna make sure to have something cooked for you for dinner."

"Don't worry about what time I will be back. I'm gonna leave some money for you to order takeout. My errands shouldn't take that long; maybe just a couple of hours. I will be back before you know it." He kissed Royal on his forehead then kissed her on the forehead before rushing out the front door. The door was slammed before Mia could even tell him that she loved him and to be careful. Mia looked at the clock on her cell phone and saw that it was after two o'clock. She locked the front door and laid down like she was told. Not even a full half hour had passed before she had fallen asleep.

Chapter Eight
Secrets Surface

Mia had been sleeping on and off for hours and now, she was up again. This time it was time to feed Royal. She looked at her cell phone and saw that it was a little after four in the morning. She quickly jumped up and checked her phone to see if Lamar had been trying to reach her. Nothing. Not a missed call nor a text from him. Sonya, however, had texted her and told her she couldn't wait to get back home to them.

Mia walked up to the crib and picked a crying Royal up. It wasn't a loud cry, thankfully, but she still didn't wanna hear it. She lifted her shirt and pulled out her nipple, and placed in his mouth. Lucky for her he latched on pretty quickly. She decided to walk around the house and feed him. *Maybe Lamar is here already. Maybe he's in the bed sleeping* Mia thought.

She walked down the hall to their bedroom and gently pushed open the door. Lamar was definitely not in the bed nor in the house for that matter. She sucked her teeth and went back to the nursery to retrieve her cell phone. She dialed his number several times but it constantly went to voicemail. She dialed Sonya's cell phone number and prayed that she picked up the phone. She wasn't sure if Sonya was awake or not but it was worth a try.

"Hey, Mia, what's up, Boo?" Sonya said groggily into the phone.
"Hey, Sweetie, I didn't mean to wake you up but have you heard from Lamar?"
"No. I haven't heard from his since around like 7 o'clock last night when he stopped past the hospital to see me and the twins."

"So he was there? What time did he leave?"

105

Trinity

"Um, I wanna say about nine when visiting hours were over. Why, what's wrong?"

"I have been trying to call him but he's not answering and he hasn't been home all night," Mia replied beginning to cry and panic. She put the phone on speaker as she placed Royal over her shoulder to be burped.

"Well, you know he has done this before, Mia. You should just take a couple of deep breaths and calm down. There is no need to stress, sweetie. I'm sure he's okay."

"You know what? You are absolutely right, Sonya," Mia said after taking a couple of deep breaths like Sonya had recommended. The tears slowly rolled down her cheeks and the phone became silent; they were both having wandering thoughts about where Lamar was. The silence was broke. When Royal made a burping noise; both women chuckled a little.

"Oh my God was that Royal?" Sonya asked Mia.

"Well you know it wasn't me," Mia laughed sniffling her tears. She continues to talk on the phone on speaker as she laid Royal back in the room because unbeknownst to Mia, he had fallen back to sleep.
"How are you feeling, Mia?" Sonya asked after a moment of silence.

"I'm good. I'm just glad to be back home."

"And I'm glad you're back home, too. All in all, I missed you, Baby. And whatever happened in the past needs to stay there."

"I agree wholeheartedly."

"Girl," Sonya laughed and Mia joined her in laughter.

"Well I know you're happy that you get to come home today, Sonya.

"I swear I am, Baby," Sonya said excitedly. "What time will you be picking us up?"

"Well, it was supposed to be both me and Lamar. But, since he's missing in action, I guess it will just be Royal and I. Did they give you an estimated time that they will release you guys?"

"Not necessarily. They said probably no later than noon."

"That's not bad. I guess we will be there around eleven to get the three of y'all."

"Okay, cool. We will see you and Royal when you get here."

"Okay, Boo. I love you," Mia replied.
"I love you, too."

■■■

"Welp, it looks like you're all are ready to go," the nurse said after walking back into Sonya's room. She handed her the discharge papers as she watched her and Mia strap the little babies into their designated car seats. "I am most definitely ready to go home, Nurse Jenny," Sonya replied lifting Prince's car seat from off the bed.

"Oh no, no, no, no, Sweetheart. You cannot be lifting that car seat, nor can you walk out of the hospital. I have to wheel you out in a wheelchair."
"What for? I am perfectly fine and capable of walking out and carrying my child," Sonya responded with attitude.

"I understand that, Ms. Jamison, but it's hospital policy," the nurse said softly.

"Fuck y'all hospital policy," Sonya yelled.

"Calm down, Sonya, and stop giving this woman a hard time," Mia laughed a little. "Is there possibility that someone can come and help me carry the other baby and the bags out to the car?" she asked the nurse.

Trinity

"Yes, Ma'am, there is," Nurse Jenny said as she rushed out of the room. She returned momentarily pushing a wheelchair and a handsome guy following behind.

"Hello, ladies, I'm Doctor Thomas, and I will be helping to escort you ladies out. Do you have everything?" he asked Sonya.

"You bet your sweet ass I do. Let's get this show on the road," she replied climbing into the wheelchair with her bag of soiled belongings.

"Wow, you're beautiful," he said aloud to Mia.

"Thank you," Mia responded blushing.

"I know this is out the blue, but do you think I can call you sometime? I would really like to take you out and-"

"Whoa, whoa, whoa there. Slow down Speedy Gonzalez," Sonya said standing up from the wheelchair and standing between them.

"Um, excuse me, but I believe she can speak for herself."

"Yeah she can but I'm telling you now that she's already spoken for, Doc."
"Do you really have a boyfriend, Sweetheart?"

Before Mia could respond, Sonya jumped in the conversation and answered for her again. "She has a boyfriend and a girlfriend if you must know," she said smirking his way.

"Yeah whatever. Like I was saying I would really like to call you and maybe take you out sometime."

"I guess you're hard of hearing. So maybe we should just show you," Sonya said. She grabbed Mia's face and pulled it towards hers. She kissed her deeply and both the nurse and doctor gasped.

"Now, we are definitely ready to blow this popsicle joint," Sonya replied before hopping back into the wheelchair. Without uttering another word, the nurse turned and pushed Sonya out of the room; and the doctor followed carrying Prince and one of the hospital bags. Mia was the last to leave the room, making sure nothing was left behind, carrying baby Princess in the car seat, and baby Royal in his carrier, along with the other hospital bag.

****

"Can you believe the nerve of the guy?" Mia asked Sonya as they rode towards the house.

"No, I can't. I also can't believe the nerve of you either, Mia," Sonya said rolling her eyes.

"What? The nerve of me? What the hell did I do?"

"You know exactly what you did. All smiling and grinning and cheesing and shit," Sonya replied mimicking the faces Mia was making earlier that day. "Oh my God, you can't be fucking serious."

"I'm dead ass serious. But, you know what, I refuse to allow you to keep disrespecting me and Lamar. I should tell his ass you was flirting with another nigga, but I'm not."

"But I wasn't flirting. You're bugging big time, Sonya."
"Yeah, whatever, Mia. I hear the shit you're talking. Can you go pass Taco Bell over there right quick, please?" Sonya asked pointing halfway down the block.

"We are not supposed to be eating that stuff and we're breastfeeding."

"We're not supposed to be doing a lot of things but that doesn't stop you," Sonya replied sarcastically. "Besides, I'm fucking starving. The kids will be perfectly fine still drinking breast milk."

"I guess so," Mia replied turning into the Taco Bell drive-thru.

"Hi, welcome to Taco Bell. How may I help you today?"

"Yeah let me get the twelve taco box, crunchy, and a large Mountain Dew."

"Anything else for you?"

"Yeah can I have another twelve taco box the same as the first?" Mia chimed in.

"Yes, your total is $22.42. Drive to the window please."

"Thank you," they said in unison.

"What happened to not eating stuff like this?" Sonya mocked Mia.

"I think it will be okay," she replied laughing.

They paid for their food and got their food and drinks a few minutes later. The taco boxes weren't even in the car good enough before the two women started drenching them in sauce and crushing. They pulled up to the house and saw that Lamar's car was in the driveway.

"I thought you said that Lamar wasn't here, Mia?"

"He wasn't here before I left."

"Well, let's go in and surprise him."
They gathered up the babies and the bags and slowly walked into the house. Luckily, all three babies were asleep, in their car seats. They could probably have a chance to get a nap in with Lamar before they all woke up for their feedings.

The two ladies tiptoed towards their bedroom, and pushed open the door. To their surprise, Lamar wasn't there. So, they decided to check the guest room. Still, there was no sign of him.

"Where on earth do you think he could be?" Mia asked Sonya.

"I don't know, Babe. Maybe he's in the nursery."

"Doing what? The kids are with us."

"Maybe he's decorating the nursery or something for the kids," Sonya replied sincerely. They both smiled at one another and headed towards the nursery. They heard banging against the wall and figured he was hanging up either shelves or pictures or anything. They opened the door slowly and walked into the room. The smile that adorned their faces quickly faded away at the sight before them.

"What the fuck is going on?" Mia yelled at the top of her lungs.
Lamar had some chick riding him on one of the rocking chairs.
"Mia? Sonya? What's up?"

"How about you tell us what's up, Lamar? ¿Quién diablos es esta perra?" she replied to him in Spanish.

"This is, uh, the new girl I had hired to help you two out with the kids while I worked and shit," he replied standing up trying to get his clothes and stuff together. The girl shuffled around the room looking for her underwear and clothes as well.

"Oh yeah, Lamar? Well it looks like she passed your interview,"Mia replied.

"It's not even like that, Mia," Lamar said walking towards her.

"Don't you fucking touch her," Sonya said pushing him backwards.

"And where you think you going, Hoe?" Mia said as the girl tried to rapidly walk past them and out the door. She grabbed a handful of her hair and smashed her face into the wall. The girl turned to face Mia as blood trickled down her face from her nose. She ran up on Mia, only to be punched with a right hook by Sonya. The girl stumbled a little but didn't hit the floor. She punched Sonya multiple times in her stomach, busting open her stitches, and causing her to fall to the floor. She curled up in a fetal position and laid on the floor and bled out.

"You stupid cunt," Mia yelled and tackled the girl to the floor. She landed blow after blow to her face until she didn't respond anymore. She stood to her feet and went over to Sonya. "Are you okay, Baby?"

"No, Mia. I think I need to go back to the hospital," she replied moving her hand from her stomach where they had stitched her up at.

"I'll take you, Boo," Lamar responded assisting Mia in helping Sonya up from the floor.

"Don't you fucking touch me! I don't want your fucking hands on me," Sonya screamed as tears streamed down her face. Lamar made eye contact with Mia and she had so many tears falling from her eyes. She shook her head in disbelief and she and Sonya walked out of the nursery.
"Mia?" he called out to her.

"Don't Mia me, Lamar," she said turning her around. "You brought this upon yourself. You always have. I'm gonna take *our* girlfriend to the hospital and get her stitches put back in. You're gonna stay here and keep an eye on the kids. And that bitch better be gone by the time we get back."

"I don't know who y'all bitches think y'all talking to, but y'all better remember this my motherfucking house. You hoes better remember who takes care of y'all. What the fuck is wrong with y'all?" Lamar ranted on. His yelling fell onto deaf ears as Mia picked up each baby, and she and Sonya kissed all three of them, before leaving out the house. She told Sonya to wait by the door while she ran and got a rag to hold against her wound.

They got into the car and backed out of the driveway. They both looked at Lamar standing in the doorway, looking like a sad puppy, before driving down the street; heading back to the hospital.

✳✳✳✳

After three hours of being at the hospital, they had finally made it back home and to their children. They walked into the house and Lamar was all over the place. All three of the babies were crying and he was scrambling trying to figure out how to make each of them a bottle. He had Princess in his arm trying to rock her and put formula in the bottles. The two women laughed at the sight of him at least trying. They locked the front door and went over to assist him in his struggle.

"Looks like you could use a hand," Sonya said over the crying.

"Yes, please, help. Damn," she rambled on.

Sonya picked Prince up from his car seat and put a bottle in his mouth, and Mia did the same with Royal. After a while, all the babies were fed, bathed, and in their designated cribs, leaving the adults to talk.

"So who was the bitch that you had up in here earlier?" Sonya asked, crossing her arms, as soon as they sat down.

"And don't lie," Mia responded copying Sonya's stance.

"It's like this, I have been kicking it with Yolanda for a while now," Lamar began.

"And what's your definition of a while, Lamar?" Mia asked.

"Oh, about two years," he responded casually.

"Two years!" they both said simultaneously.

"Are you fucking kidding me? You kept a secret from us for two goddamn years?" Sonya asked.

"Yeah, I'm sorry."

"You don't mean that shit, Lamar. That's the exact same thing you said when you told me about her," Mia said pointing at Sonya.
"I do mean it this time."

"How many are there, Lamar? How many other women have there been?" Mia asked softly.

"You don't wanna know, Boo."

"Yeah we do," Sonya chimed in.

"Including the two of you, I have been fucking and spending time with twelve women total."

"Wow. This is fucking unbelievable. But, I can say I'm not even fucking surprised," Mia said wiping her tears away. She stood to her feet and paced around the room. "What about you, Sonya?"

"What you mean what about me?"

"What secrets are you holding back from us?"

"Well, honestly, whenever I leave here for hours at a time, I'm not going to my mother's house. I'm meeting up with my ex at a hotel."
"Wow so you fucking another nigga behind my back?" Lamar scolded at her through clenched teeth.

"Yep. Just like you fucking another bitch behind mine," she said imitating him.

"Wow okay. Well since we're all sharing secrets I got a secret of my own," Mia said aloud. "I been fucking John John." Lamar and Sonya exchanged looks at one another. Lamar stood up and walked over to Mia. "You wanna repeat that again, Mia?"

"You heard exactly what the fuck I said, Nigga. I said I'm fucking John John," she said closer to his ear. Without thinking, he grabbed Mia up by her throat and started choking her profusely.

"Lamar let her go," Sonya screamed jumping off the couch. She and Mia both tried their best to pry his fingers from around Mia's neck, but he wasn't budging.

Sonya ran and grabbed the gun from under the mattress. She shot a round through the ceiling and all the commotion had ceased.

"Cut that shit out now! Both of you," Sonya yelled. "We all been fucking up and cheating on each other. We knew what the fuck we were doing. But now we need to put our differences aside and come together for these fucking kids. We need to stop these shenanigans. We all love each other or we wouldn't be here. And if you don't wanna be here, you can freely walk out the door," she said pointing towards the front door.

"I'm sorry, Mia. You, too, Sonya," Lamar said kissing each one of them. "I'm sorry, too," Mia replied.

"Me, too," Sonya chimed in. She kissed Mia and Mia kissed her back. Before you knew it, they were all stripping each other out of their clothes and fondling one another. What started in the living went to the kitchen, then ended in the bedroom. The makeup love making session lasted for a total of two hours between the three lovers. They all had fallen asleep with Lamar in the middle, and Mia and Sonya on each side of him.

Trinity

Around 3 o'clock in the morning, the static from the baby monitor stirred Sonya awake. She groggily rose up from the bed and slipped on a nightshirt and slippers, before heading to the nursery. Upon arrival, she saw that Princess had awaken. She picked the baby up and checked her diaper. She quickly changed her pamper and grabbed one of the already made formula bottles that she had gotten from the nurse at the hospital. She had sat in the rocking chair opposite the one that Lamar had fucked Yolanda on because they haven't had a chance to sterilize it just yet. Princess gulped down the the entire four ounce bottle within ten minutes and then burped quickly. Sonya held her in her arms and rocked her back and forth in the chair as she sang her a lullaby in Spanish.

A la nanita nana nanita ella, nanita ella
Mi niña tiene sueño, bendito sea, bendito sea
A la nanita nana nanita ella, nanita ella
Mi niña tiene sueño, bendito sea, bendito sea
Fuentecita que corre clara y sonora
Ruiseñor que en la selva
Cantando y llora
Calla mientras la cuna se balancea
A la nanita nana nanita ella
A la nanita nana nanita ella, nanita ella
Mi niña tiene sueño, bendito sea, bendito sea
Fuentecita que corre clara y sonora
Ruiseñor que en la selva
Cantando y llora
Calla mientras la cuna se balancea
A la nanita nana nanita ella!

After she had finish singing her lullaby, Princess was fast asleep in her arms. She slowly rose to her feet and walked over to the crib. She kissed Princess on her forehead then laid her down gently on the comforter that lined the crib. She checked on the other babies to make sure they were okay before exiting the room. She pulled the door up a little not closing it all the way just in case.

"Is everything okay, Sonya?" Mia asked as Sonya walked back into the room.

"Yeah everything is good. Princess had waken up and needed some attention. That's all," she replied deciding she would lay up under Mia rather than get on the opposite side of Lamar again.

"What about Royal and Prince? Did they wake up, too?"

"Girl no. You know that if all three were awake I would have woke y'all asses up, too," Sonya laughed in a low tone.

"I hear you. Well, I'm going back to sleep. Good night, Sweetie."
"Good night, love," Sonya replied kissing Mia's soft lips. She stroked Mia's hair until she had fallen asleep. Not long after, Sonya had fallen back into a deep slumber as well.

✶✶✶✶

"I still cannot believe what the fuck went down the other day," Mia said to Sonya as they were riding in the car. They were spending their first day out with the kiddies since Lamar was working. Well, at least that's what he said to them.

"Girl, what are you talking about?"

"That shit with Lamar and Hoelanda."

"I'm right there with you. That nigga really lost his fucking mind trying to play us like a couple of fools," Sonya added.

"I'm not gonna play the fool for his ass anymore."

"Me either."

"We need to find us some men that will appreciate good women like us."

117   Trinity

"I agree. But where will we find niggas like that?" Sonya asked chuckling.

"Hell I don't know. How did you meet Lamar?"

"Well, I, um, met him at the movies?"

"At the movies? Really?"

"Yeah. I was out with this guy and Lamar had seen us walking to the car after the movie had ended. I had noticed him earlier that evening but thought he was just waiting for someone. But, anyway, he approached us and told me that he can do anything I want him to do better than the guy I was on the date with. So, to be funny and see what his response was, I let the guy's hand go and asked Lamar if he would eat my pussy good. His reply was 'I will have you flowing like Niagara Falls.' Then I asked if he eat ass and he said 'like groceries.' My last question was did he have a girlfriend and he told me that was none of my concern. So, I grabbed his arm and went on with him. From then on, that was my man," Sonya replied grinning from ear to ear.

"You mean my man that you were cheating with?"

"Technically no because I knew nothing about you until a few years ago around the time he introduced us to one another."

"Yeah whatever."

Sonya parked the car and they took out Royal's single stroller and Prince and Princess's double stroller. They were both looking fly and ready to shop a little. Lucky for them, instead of having the kids Christmas Day, they had given birth a couple weeks before. So, they were kind of appreciative for that.

For three hours, they were in and out of stores and running back and forth to the car. This last go 'round they had to split up so they could get each other's gifts. They had already gotten Lamar and the babies out the way so they were all good.

After about forty-five minutes of shopping alone, the two ladies met up again in the food court. They changed all three infants then headed to the food court for some grub. They both took turns watching the kids while they other ordered food. As they ate, they fed the kids as well. Sonya thought it was gonna be a little difficult because she had twins, but she was wrong. She propped up the blankets a little and placed the bottle on top of them in their mouths. After they finished, the babies were burped and placed back in the car seat stroller combos.

"So what did you get me, Boo?" Sonya asked Mia after finishing the last of her food.

"Don't be asking questions. You will find out in a few days."
"You fucking suck."

"No shit, Sherlock," Mia replied. They both burst out in laughter.

They hit up a couple more stores before heading back home. It was nearing six o'clock and they had to get dinner ready for their man.

Chapter Nine

Merry Christmas

T he Temptations Christmas album was blaring through the surround speakers throughout the house. Sonya and Mia had spent the past couple of days decorating the house and making it look as festive as they could for the family. Both Mia and Sonya were kind of skeptical to have their mothers there, but it was the holidays. They looked around at everyone in the room. They were dancing, drinking egg nog, eating plates of food, and playing with the babies. They were surprised their mothers were being on their best behaviors, especially Mia's mother, Tonya. Lord knows how much she hated Lamar after the incident at the hospital. Ms. Tonya continued to have hated Lamar for what he had done to her daughter.

"The house looks beautiful and the food is great," Ms. Tonya said to Sonya and her daughter.

"Thanks, Ms. Jacobs. We worked really hard," Sonya replied.

"Thanks, Ma."

"Have you two had a chance to open your Christmas presents from me yet?"

"No," the two women responded simultaneously.

"Well, what are you waiting for?" Ms. Tonya laughed.

"Where are they anyway?" Mia asked her mother.

"I snuck them in the bedroom. Let's go," she said. She grabbed them both by the hand and scurried to the bedroom. She closed the door and made sure to lock it before they opened their gift boxes.

"Oh wow," Mia replied.

"These are nice," Sonya replied in addition.

"Do y'all really like them?" Tonya asked.

"Yes we do, Ma."

The two ladies pulled out of the box a pair of handcuffs and matching teddies that were in different colors. Mia had a red lace teddy, while Sonya had a green lace one.

"I'm glad you both love them. Really puts you in the holiday spirit," Tonya chuckled.

"I can't wait to put this on. And I have some sexy pumps that will go perfect with this."

"I knew it was a good idea to buy some when we were at the mall the other day. I got some cute little boots that will go nice with mine as well."
"I'm just ecstatic that you both love your presents. Just don't bring anymore babies around anytime soon," Tonya laughed. The three women laughed together and exchanged hugs. They were heading out the room but Tonya stopped Mia and asked her to stay behind for a minute so they could talk. She agreed and told Sonya she would be out in a second. They exchanged a kiss and Sonya left and Mia shut the door behind her.

"What's up, Ma?"

"Are you really happy in this situation, Mia?" she blurted out to her daughter without hesitation.

121   Trinity

Mia laughed before responding. "Mom, I have told you a million times that I'm happy. We all are. I love them and they love me."

"But what about all that I hate stuff you were talking when he put your little tail out the house? I really thought you were done with these shenanigans. And then you had the nerve to stay with him after he cheated on you with that other woman recently. And with Sonya and the other women. Or, have you forgotten all that happened?"

"See this is exactly why I don't tell you anything about my life, Mom. You're always throwing shit up in my face that I talk to you about," Mia replied rolling her eyes and making her way to the bedroom door.

Tonya grabbed her by the arm. "You better watch your tongue little girl and remember I'm your goddamn mother," she said through clenched teeth. "I'm just looking out for your best interest like a mother supposed too. Just leave him, Mia. You and Sonya both. You both are young and still have your whole lives ahead of you. I guarantee there is someone out their for you that will be willing to accept you and my grandson; the same goes for Sonya."

"We have all already hashed out our differences and we are doing better now, Ma. Would you just please give it a rest?" Mia snatched her arm away from her mother's grasp and walked out the room.

"Lord, please help my child to see the light. I know she will be punished and at this point she needs to be. She is so darn stubborn. I just need you to open her eyes to realize she is sleeping with the devil himself and his mistress. Amen." She walked out the room and closed the door behind her.

✳✳✳✳

The Christmas party and dinner continued to go on. Other then the conversation that had transpired between Mia and Tonya, no other mishaps had aroused and the evening was going great. Princess, Royal, and Prince had gotten so many presents from everyone you would have thought they were having another baby shower.

"Where are we going to put all of this stuff?" Sonya asked laughing.

"We will find a place I'm sure," Lamar replied. He had opened all of his gifts and loved every last one of them. Mia had gotten him the latest Air Jordans and an Armani watch to match. Sonya bought him a pair of diamond earrings, diamond cuff links with his initials on them, and a diamond encrusted Rolex to match. After everybody had finished exchanging their presents amongst each other, Lamar stood to present his to Sonya and Mia. "May I have everyone's attention, please?" he said aloud. Everyone stopped their chatter and gave him their undivided attention. "Thank you. I wanna thank you all for coming out to celebrate Christmas with us and have dinner with us. It's now my turn to present my two beautiful girlfriends with their Christmas presents." He walked over to the mantle and pulled out two square boxes that looked to be identical. He walked back over and instructed both Mia and Sonya to close their eyes and hold out their hands. They did as they were told and tried their best to contain their excitement. On the count of three, open your eyes and open your gifts. Okay?"

"Okay," they said in unison.

"One, two, three. Open your eyes," he said.

They both opened their eyes and boxes at the same time and gasped. They both had matching necklaces with their and Lamar's initials on them, matching four carat diamond rings, and a key on a key ring."
"Oh my God. These are beautiful," Mia replied.

"Yeah they are," Sonya added.

"Glad you both like your gifts. Now I would like an answer from both of you." They both looked at him and waited. "I love the both of you and I ask for the both of your hands in marriage."

123   Trinity

"Yes!" they both squealed. The women both hopped up on their feet and ran over to Lamar. They kissed him and hugged him and did the same to each other. The room was surrounded with clapping, congratulating, and tears; except for Tonya and Amelia. They were not too thrilled. They looked at each other and knew they had to do damage control. Before they could make their move, they stopped and looked at how happy their daughters looked.

"We can't take away their happiness," Tonya said.

"Like hell we can't," Amelia responded getting up but Tonya held her back.

"What good will that do? They will just hate and resist us."

Amelia looked at her daughter and noticed she had never seen her so happy before. "I guess you're right. But this isn't over."

"I couldn't agree with you more, Amelia," Tonya responded. They put on fake smiles and picked up their champagne flutes to go and congratulate their daughters and future son-in-law, Lamar.

✳✳✳✳

"Well, well, well, what do we do now?" Mia asked Lamar and Sonya.
"Not sure. Everybody's gone home and the babies are asleep for the night," Sonya replied.

"I got something in mind," Lamar said. He put on a slow jams cd and danced with his fiancées. He dipped and twirled them and kissed them all over. He was in love.

How could a nigga like me be in love? Especially with two beautiful women? How did I get to be so damn lucky? He thought to himself.
"How about a movie?" Mia said after awhile.

"What you wanna watch, Bae?" Sonya asked.

124

"Home Alone," she said cheesing hard.

"You are such a big ass kid," Sonya replied.

"Screw you. You know that's my favorite movie."

"We know," Lamar and Sonya said in unison.
The trio grabbed a couple of snacks and popped some popcorn to get ready for a movie night.

Everything was going great and they were all enjoying each other's company. Around one in the morning there was a knock at the door. *Who in the hell could that be?* Lamar thought. He excused himself and got up from the sofa. He grabbed his gun just in case he needed it, and headed towards the front door while the girls ducked down on the floor in front of the couch out of sight.

"Yo, who that is?" he asked looking through the peephole; gun already cocked and ready.

"It's me, Sam, fool," said the voice on the other side of the door.
A few locks clicked, and the front door opened. Stepping through the front door was an image of sin. Mia and Sonya both gawked at the sight of Sam. But they made sure not to let Lamar know they were looking.
Sam, short for Samson, was tall as hell, literally almost seven feet. His blonde locs reached the middle of his back, and prison tatts adorned his muscular body. He walked into the house and Lamar offered him a seat on the loveseat.

"Sam, these are my fiancées, Mia and Sonya."

"Fiancées? Damn okay. How y'all doing?"

"We're good," they both said smiling. Lamar picked up on it but brushed it off. He focused his attention back to Sam.

125   Trinity

"What's good with you, Bro?" Lamar asked Sam as he sat down.

"Man, ain't shit. I just need somewhere to crash for about a week."

"Well you know mi casa es su casa, Brody."

"Respect."

"What happened, man? Thought you was staying with your old lady out in Bmore?"

"Shit I was. She caught me an ole girl from out PA fucking while she was supposed to be at work. She came home and caught us fucking and I mean hard."

"That's crazy. Welp everybody can't be as lucky as me and have two ladies," he said leaning back and putting his around both of their shoulders. He gave them both a peck on the lips and they giggled like two school girls. "Man I swear you got it made. You got two fine bad bitches on your arm. I envy you," Sam laughed and dapped up Lamar. Lamar told Sonya and Mia to get the guest room ready for Sam and they did as they were told and then went into their room. Meanwhile, Lamar and Sam continued to talk and joke around in the living room for another hour.

"Did you check out how fine Sam is?" Sonya asked.

"Girl yes," Mia giggled.

"I wish I could get me a piece of that."

"As do I, Sonya. As do I," Mia replied. The two women talked a little longer before they took a quick shower and laid down for the night. After awhile, Lamar crawled into bed and joined his women.

****

Mia crept out the room in the middle of the night to go and check on the kids. They were all still sound asleep with their pacifiers in their mouths. She was heading back to her room to her lovers when she bumped into Sam coming out the hallway bathroom.

"Sorry, Sam. I should have watched where I was going," Mia said shyly.

"You're perfectly fine, Mia, right?"

"Yeah that's me."

"Yeah you are definitely fine," he repeated as he ran the tip of his index down her arm. The mix of his touch and the smell of his Burberry cologne woke her pussy up and it started to drip in her lace thong she had under her satin robe.

"Um, I gotta go before Lamar or Sonya realize I'm, uh, not in the bed," she stammered after she remembered all she had on under her robe were the stringy panties and nothing else.

Sam put his finger to her lips and pushed her against the wall. He pulled on the ribbon of the robe that kept it closed and opened it up, exposing her beautiful brown breasts and big dark areolas. He licked around her areola before putting a nipple in his mouth. He ran his fingertips down her stomach and over her belly button, as he made his way inside her underwear. She gasped loudly and he threw his free hand over her mouth. He stopped sucking on her nipple and then got on his knees, throwing her thigh over his shoulder. He pulled her thong to the side and slipped his tongue in her hot pussy. He flicked it back and forth across her clit and continued to finger her. She squirmed and wanted to push him away but it was feeling too damn good. Once she squirted, he cleaned up his mess and stood up. He licked his fingers, looked her in the eyes smiling then went back into the guest room.

Trinity

What the hell was that? Mia thought. She slipped into the bathroom and wiped her pussy and inner thighs with a damp washcloth. She tiptoed as quietly as possible back towards the room, but she got busted by Sonya in the hall. "Where the hell were you at all this time?" Sonya said a little above a whisper.

"Shhh. I went to go check on the kids," Mia replied.

"Mmhmm sure you did," Sonya said not believing a word she was saying.

"I know you were in there with Sam."

"What? No I wasn't."

"If you say so but I know my eyes didn't deceive me, Mia." With that being said, Sonya retreated back to their room with an embarrassed Mia treading slowly behind. She tried to kiss Sonya good night but Sonya turned her back towards her. Before long, they both had fallen back to sleep.

Chapter Ten
Happy New Year

The past couple of days were a little hard for Mia. She had to actually walk around the house as casual and as normal as possible without letting on that something happened between her and Sam. Lamar would kill her if he had found out. Hell, he would probably kill them both if it came down to it. Mia wasn't too worried about Sonya saying anything because she knows she and Sam have had their own little rendezvous. Mia and Sam were in the living room just chilling waiting for Sonya to get ready. They had to take the babies for a doctor visit and, as usual, Lamar was not in attendance. Instead, he asked Sam to chauffeur us there as if we didn't have cars of our own.

"Yo, we still good, Mia?" Sam blurted out the blue.

"Yeah, yeah, we're cool. We are definitely cool," Mia rambled on.

"Um, okay, then why are you acting the way you do around me?"

"No reason, Sam. I'm just not used to another guy being around the house so much, that's all."

"That's all?"

"Yep."

"Are you sure?"

"I said 'yes', Sam, shit," she snapped.

"Okay. I won't bring it up anymore," he said getting up from the couch and going to the kitchen. "Psycho bitch," he mumbled under his breath. Mia had heard him but she ain't have time for his foolishness.

It was the day before New Years Eve and they still had to go get a bottle of champagne and food for tomorrow night. She had just finished bundling up Royal, Princess, and Prince and strapping them in their car seats. She looked at them in awe at how wide-eyed and alert they were. For only being a few weeks old, they all looked as though they had even grown a little. Her heart was warm with love and a gentle smile grew on her face. She stood to her feet and was heading to get Sonya but she was coming out to them. "Sorry it took so long, Babe. I couldn't find my Timbs for shit so I had to settle for my Nike boots."

Mia examined Sonya's outfit. "You look great, Boo. I think the Nike boots look better with that coat anyway."

"Cool. You two ready to go?" she asked looking in the direction of Sam. "I been ready. I was just waiting for y'all," Sam responded walking over to them. They all picked up a car seat and both diaper bags and headed out the door.

"To the doctor we go," Sonya said loudly in a joking manner.

"This shit is about to suck. I don't want my baby getting no damn shots," Mia said sincerely.

"Me neither but that's some shit we gotta do."

"I know."

"Then let's go."

They strapped the babies in Sam's truck securely before heading to the doctor's office.

✳✳✳✳

Surprisingly, the visit to the doctor's office didn't go to bad. Other than the long wait, they were quick and out by two o'clock.

"Where we headed to now?" Sam asked the ladies after they were all back in the truck and buckled up for safety.

"We're hungry," Sonya replied.

"Me, too. Can we go to Chipotle?" Mia asked from the third row of the big Suburban.

"Shit I can go for that, too," Sam said in agreement.

"Well let's hurry up before I have to start drinking formula," Sonya said. They all laughed as Sam headed to Chipotle.

They got to the restaurant and was glad to see a short line. They were able to get their food and be out in less than ten minutes.

"So, have you thought about your New Year's resolution yet?" Sam asked Sonya trying to start up a conversation as they headed to the car. Mia had stayed in the car and Sonya ordered her food for her.

"I surely did and I hope it happens."

"I'm sure it will."

The next two stops were quick in and out stops to the grocery store and the liquor store. They decided on cooking pork ribs, collard greens, macaroni and cheese, and cornbread for dinner tomorrow. And since Sonya was a champagne connoisseur, she picked up a bottle of Armand de Brignac Ace of Spades Brut Rose that totaled $450 for them to toast in a new year. They arrived home an hour later and Lamar was pulling up right behind them. He hopped out his all white Bentley and kissed his girls, then dapped up his mans. He helped them take the car seats and bags in the house. Lamar was feeling some type of way when he seen Sam, Mia, and Sonya pulling out Chipotle bowls. Before he had a chance to curse all of them out, Sonya handed him his bowl. He kissed her and they all dug in as they watched a basketball game.

The evening ended earlier than expected for the trio plus one. Sam and Lamar decided last minute to go to the bar around eleven. By then, all three kids were wide awake and ready to wreak havoc on their moms. Lamar kissed his family of five before heading out.

"I love being a parent," Mia said as she breastfed Royal.

"Me, too. I have been happy in my life but nothing compares to how I feel about being a mother. And then I'm a mother of twins," Sonya explained. She had Princess sucking milk from her breast and Prince was drinking his share of breast milk from a bottle.

They had played with the kids and took endless pictures of them and with them and posted them on social media. As it neared two o'clock in the morning, the babies had fallen back to sleep. Sonya and Mia decided to follow them and go to bed as well. They tucked them all in bed and decided on laying in their room in the corner with oversized pillows. They got under a blanket and cuddled.

Instead of going to sleep, Mia start playing with Sonya's nipples under her camisole.

"Mmmm. What you doing baby?" she asked moaning and turning over to face Mia.

"I want you to ride my face and let your juices run down my cheeks," Mia replied moving her hand down to Sonya's panties and slipping two fingers inside her wet walls.

Sonya got up and Mia scooted down to lay flat on her back. Sonya positioned herself over Mia's mouth. Mia pulled her panties to the side and pulled Sonya down on her face. She licked and sucked on Sonya's clit and pussy until she squirted. Mia had Sonya's sweet nectar running down the side of her face, a little slipping into her ear. She continued until Sonya tapped out.

"My turn," Sonya said after she caught her breath. They switched positions and Sonya did the same to Mia that had gotten done to here. After about an hour of pleasing each other, they wiped their faces with some diaper wipes and laid down. This time they were really going to sleep.

✳✳✳✳✳

The next day had come and was damn near coming to an end. They had a smooth running day today. There was no arguing or disagreements amongst the lovers for once. Sam had enjoyed himself as well, but after dinner he had to leave but he told Lamar that he would be back.

"Damn, you ain't gonna bring in the new year with me and my ladies, Bro?"

"Yeah, Bro. I just gotta run past this shawty house right quick."

"True shit. Well see you when you get back."

"Peace," Sam said rushing out the front door.

"Well it's almost 11:30, ladies. We can have us a quickie if you want. Hell, we can go until after midnight, too," Lamar laughed.

"You go ahead to the bedroom and get ready. Sonya and I will get ready in the bathroom," Mia said kissing him seductively. Sonya followed in tow and did the same before following Mia into the bedroom, and disappearing into the bathroom.

133

"Y'all hurry up in there," Lamar yelled. He had given them a few minutes before he went in the room. On the bed he saw two pairs of handcuffs. *Oh this gonna be good* he thought to himself. He stripped out his clothes and wore nothing but boxers. He hopped on the bed and called for the girls to come out again.

The two women rose from the bathroom wearing the matching teddies that Mia's mother had bought them for Christmas.
"Wow," was all Lamar could say.

Mia and Sonya kissed him and then instructed him to lie in the middle of the bed. They both grabbed a pair of handcuffs and cuffed his hands and feet to the bedposts.

"Are you ready?" Sonya asked in her sultry tone.

"Damn straight," Lamar responded excitedly.

"I hope so," Mia added.
They both reached under the mattress and pulled out a gun.

"Yo, what the fuck is going on?" he said struggling to free his hands and feet.

"Don't do that, L, or you will cut your wrists," Mia told him.

"What the fuck is going on?" he repeated.

"It's a little thing called karma. You see, karma is a bitch and she is here to ruin your life," Sonya said.

"What the hell is that supposed to mean? What karma?"

"For all the years of hell you put us through, Lamar. Don't act like you don't know," Sonya responded.

"All in all, Lamar, we love you so much but we are tired of the disrespect, the abuse, and everything else you do to us under the son," Mia said through tears, cocking her gun.

"I took care of you two ungrateful bitches. I'm all y'all got."

"Correction our children are all we have," Mia replied aiming her gun at him.

"Whoa, whoa, Mia not yet. But, we are gonna kill him. I think we should let him in on our little secret though. Since we're gonna kill him anyway, he can at least take this information to the grave with him. Don't you think so, Baby?" Mia nodded her head in agreement."

"What fucking secret? Just let me go. You don't have to kill me," he pleaded.

"Oh shut the fuck up, Lamar," Sonya spat. "You are gonna die and there's nothing else to say about it. You treated us along with other women like shit. And for that, you need to go meet your maker. But before you go, this secret we have been hiding for years is about to blow your fucking mind," she laughed.

"Spit that shit out already, Hoe."
"Name calling, Lamar? Really?" Sonya hit him across the head with the butt of the gun and laid down on the bed beside him. "I'm gonna let Mia tell you, Baby."

"Well to be honest, I knew all about Sonya before you ever introduced us."
"The fuck is you talking about, Mia?" he asked.

"Exactly what I said. Sonya didn't meet you on accident. It was all a part of our plan to take you for everything we could. Sonya is actually a friend of mine from high school and we have been doing this to niggas for years. Our mothers know everything and they were with the shits as well. We just didn't know it would come to the point of you proposing to us. But I do love this ring and I will be wearing this rock," she said examining her engagement ring. They heard the front door open and close followed by heavy footsteps.

"Help me, help me." Lamar yelled at the top of his lungs.
"Shut the fuck up before I shoot your ass right now," Sonya said pressing the gun into Lamar's forehead.

Sam came around the corner with his gun drawn. "What the hell is this?" he asked the women. He looked at Lamar and saw the gash on his face from the gun. "Dawg, what's going on?"

"These bitches are trying to kill me, man. Help me, Bro."

Sam looked back and forth between Mia and Sonya then back at Lamar. "They are not going to kill you, L. You're tripping," Sam laughed.

"What the fuck is so damn funny? I'm telling you the truth."

"They aren't gonna kill you. I am," Sam replied. His smile dropped from his face and was replaced with a face more sinister.

"You? You really gonna kill me, Bro?"

"Yep."
Pop. Pop. Pop.

Three shots rang out, echoing throughout the house. Sam, Mia, and Sonya hurried to clean up the mess and stuff Lamar's body in the trunk of Sam's truck. Mia put Royal and his clothes and stuff in her car and Sonya did the same with the twins's things in her car. Everything else they would come back for.

They followed Sam to Anacostia park to dump Lamar's body in the putrid waters.

"Any last words, ladies?" Sam asked.

"See you in hell," Mia replied.

"Happy New Year, Baby," Sonya said.

"Bet." Sam dropped the body in the water and grabbed ahold of their hands.

"To our new beginning," Sam said as they walked back to their vehicles. They were now headed to the new house that Lamar had bought them to live in.

They couldn't wait to get to their new town and find a new sucker. Hopefully it will only lasts months rather than years the next time.

About The Author

American author Rachelle Jarred was born in Washington, D.C. and currently works full-time as the CEO of BluGem Publishing, where her books are published. She has been entranced by the magic of written words and had an unflinching love for writing since she was seven, and now lives her dream of being a published author and a poet. Writing is more than just her career; it's her way of life.

Rachelle prides herself on exploring multiple fiction genres. With sizzling hot erotica, blood-cuddling horror, and scintillating suspense, she has enticing packages for every book lover. She is looking forward to diving into children's stories in the near future.

Between her writing career and her life as a mother of two, Rachelle enjoys spending time with her loved ones and always makes time to help new authors find their way in the writing industry. She currently resides in Prince George's County, Maryland.

Trinity

www.ingramcontent.com/pod-product-compliance
Lightning Source LLC
Chambersburg PA
CBHW071924220626

47052CB00002B/453